MW01124136

Dedicated To My Mother:
Judy Claire Richardson (1942-2000)

The Grappler

William K. Richardson

Order this book online at www.trafford.com
or email orders@trafford.com

Most Trafford titles are also available at major online book retailers.

Printed in the United States of America.

ISBN: 978-1-4269-6035-2 (sc)
ISBN: 978-1-4269-6036-9 (e)

Trafford rev. 03/26/2011

www.trafford.com

North America & international
toll-free: 1 888 232 4444 (USA & Canada)
phone: 250 383 6864 • fax: 812 355 4082

— One —

Life at the new school in the new city began as life at his old school in his old city ended: in the school's office, awaiting a meeting with the principal. There was one big difference. Jamal wasn't in trouble now; he hadn't time to find any. Heck, he had just registered at Kennedy High School, his new high school in Memphis. After registering his grandson Jamal Hayes for school, Lonny Hayes requested a meeting with the school's principal, Mr. Griffith. This was a first for Jamal: being in the principal's office for "unofficial business." The meeting was his grandfather's idea. "Get you off on the right foot," he had said.

As Jamal and his grandfather sat in the main office's waiting area, typical school day business occurred around them. Students entered the office, asking questions of Mrs. Fitzpatrick, the school's secretary. She alternately answered their questions and answered her phone, which seemed to ring the minute she finished with a student. A small office to the right of the waiting area was filled with a parent, student and the guidance counselor. Jamal heard something about college loans or scholarships.

Jamal sat quietly. He had no idea what his grandfather had in mind with meeting the principal. He was certain, however, it had something to do with rules and cracking down on Jamal, making his life at Kennedy much like life at his new home, his grandfather's: rules and work. Lonny Hayes was in his 50s, and Jamal thought the man to be "old school" to an extreme. He had only been at the man's house one week, yet it seemed like a year. On Jamal's first day at his grandfather's, he wasn't even allowed to unpack his things before his grandfather informed, "The damn vacation is over." What vacation, Jamal thought? Day to day life on Chicago's south side was many things, but it could hardly be considered to be a vacation. Hawaii, it was certainly not. Jamal would soon find out what his grandfather meant; life with granddad would be filled with chores and a schedule for everything. Free time – "idle ways," his grandfather called it – would not exist in large doses.

And his grandfather meant it.

That first week in Memphis, Jamal didn't go to school. It was the week of Thanksgiving, and school was only in session one and half days. The entire week, Thanksgiving Day and Sunday included, consisted of labor, his own labor: cleaning up around the house, raking leaves in the front and back yards, bagging up the leaves, climbing on the roof and clearing all the gutters of trash, cleaning out and rearranging the garage, washing his grandfather's work truck and "weekend" car, and helping his grandfather with his home improvement side-job, on a Saturday, no less.

Though Sunday was a day for worship at his grandfather's (and now his) Baptist church, work even found Jamal there, as the pastor and Jamal's grandfather had him move some new furniture into the church's office and Sunday school classroom.

Lonny Virgil Hayes was a demanding man, and now this man was 15-year-old Jamal's guardian. Didn't "guardian" mean "guard" or "protect?" In the case of his grandfather, the word meant "drill sergeant" or "task master."

Before Sunday night of that first week, Jamal never thought he would look forward to going to school, but, with calluses covering his hands as he sat at the Sunday dinner table, he found he couldn't wait for Monday morning to arrive and his first day at his new school to begin. Anything was better than his new home and all the work and rules of his grandfather.

Yet, here he sat, with his grandfather, in the school office. School, it appeared, wouldn't provide any rest from the watchful eye of his grandfather.

Jamal's thoughts were interrupted by the voice of Ms. Fitzpatrick: "Mr. Hayes, Mr. Griffith will see you now. She had a nice smile and voice. Jamal thought this might be the last nice thing anyone would say to him.

Lonny and Jamal made their way through the small gate that separated the small waiting area from the area behind the long office counter. The two entered the office, and Jamal took a seat, only to have his grandfather smack him in the back of the head: "Boy, get up and wait until you are invited to sit."

"Mr. Hayes, it's a pleasure to meet you," said Mr. Griffith, offering his hand to his grandfather. "I take it this is Jamal?" The same hand – huge to Jamal – was extended to Jamal. He nervously shook it.

"Have a seat gentlemen," said Mr. Griffith, as he shut the office door and took his place behind his desk in a large leather chair. The man was big. He had to be 6'5" or so, thought Jamal. Jamal looked at the many photos on the walls of the office. One was a team photo of a football team, a championship team. Mr. Griffith was a coach on the team. Another photo showed a Chicago Bears player, #77, tackling a player from the Detroit Lions. Though he couldn't see the player's face too well, Jamal thought the #77 to be Mr. Griffith; the man was surely big enough. (He would later find out that #77 indeed was Mr. Griffith.)

Jamal's viewing was interrupted by Mr. Griffith's voice: "Mr. Hayes, in preparation for this meeting, I had guidance keep Jamal's file for me after he registered this morning. You asked for a meeting, and I thought it would be helpful to see the hand Kennedy was dealt when it registered Jamal. After viewing his file, I can't say that I'm overly impressed."

"No reason to be impressed. Boy was out of control in Chicago. Why his mama sent him to me. It's why I wanted this meeting with you. I ain't for no nonsense, and I want this one here watched and forced in the right direction. You can count on seeing me once a week. His mama sent him to me to get him right, and I aim to do just that."

With each word, Jamal felt smaller and smaller, much smaller than his 5'7" 160 pound self. When would this meeting end? When would all the talking about him and the staring at him end?

"I'll be here," Jamal's grandfather continued. "Count on it, but if this boy here gets out of line and acts up, just put that board on his butt, and then call me, and I'll do it double. Jamal may have done as he wanted in Chicago, but he'll do as *I want* in Memphis. Too many young boys getting' locked up and dead. If someone had taken a belt or board to their rear-ends, might've saved them. This one ain't goin' down that road."

"Well. Let's hope it doesn't come to that," said Mr. Griffith, adding, "but it can be arranged if that is what you want." Looking toward Jamal, he asked, "Jamal, what do you think? What do you have to say?"

Silence. Jamal couldn't wait to get out of this office. Even Algebra sounded better than this …what was that word he learned in history…. inquisition…that's it: "a severe interrogation." He remembered it as some religious thing in Europe. It wasn't a good thing, and he was in the middle of one. Just say what they want to hear, and he would be on his way. Any conversation with the words "board" and his "backside" was not good and could be an inquisition.

"I'm gonna' do right," Jamal sheepishly answered. "I don't want to be in the office in trouble and stuff."

"That's good," Griffith said. "Of course, that's entirely up to you. Do the right thing, and you won't be in here. I try to keep things simple for my students here at Kennedy. Do three things, and you won't have problems with me: come to school, get your lessons done, and show respect to the staff. Simple. Do these things. No problem. Do otherwise. Big problems, namely me."

"I want to do good here." Jamal hoped Memphis was like Chicago. Say what is expected to the adults, and then move on and go about your business like had been. Something told him it might not be that easy with Griffith. It certainly didn't work with his grandfather.

Mr. Griffith met Jamal's words with his own: "And I want you to do well, and the entire staff, as well as your grandfather wants you to do well. We are all here to help you, but, first and foremost, it is up to you."

Lonny Hayes jumped right in saying, "That's right, Jamal. We're here to help, but it's you that's got to do the heavy lifting. It's your schooling, not mine or Mr. Griffith's. This is a fresh start for you. It's up to you how this turns out."

"Exactly," agreed Mr. Griffith, "this is a fresh start, which means you get a clean slate. What happened in Chicago stays in Chicago. It's over and done. No one here knows about Chicago, and they don't have to know. You're a bright boy. Though your grades are nothing to brag about, your test scores indicate a good mind in that head of yours. Just hasn't been used a lot. Who knows what you can do? Apply yourself, and you might find that school is not such a bad place. You might even like it."

Jamal's grandfather arose from his chair, extending his hand to Mr. Griffith: "Mr. Griffith, once again, good to meet you. I'll be seeing more of you. I have to get to work. Any problems, don't hesitate to call."

"It's a pleasure to meet you also, Mr. Hayes. Don't worry about Jamal. Let us do that, and we'll get him on down the road."

Jamal got up to leave, but Mr. Griffith told him to keep his seat. What now, Jamal thought. He continued to sit. What, more lecturing?

After seeing his grandfather out, Mr. Griffith returned to his office, closing the door. The man was even bigger than he appeared earlier. "Jamal, I wanted to have a little chat without your grandfather present, a man to man chat with just you and me before you went to your remaining classes today." He picked up the phone and pushed a button or two and said, "Mrs. Fitzpatrick, find out what class Derrick Slater is in and have him come to my office."

Who is this Derrick Slater? What's he got to do with me? Jamal silently asked himself.

"Jamal, I have my own little program, something I created to help new students adjust to Kennedy High School. It isn't easy being the new kid at school. I've found it can help to pair up new student with older students, students who can help mentor and guide them around the first few weeks. Kind of like a big brother or sister to show the new student around and introduce them to the school. It's like a first friend here. You'll like Derrick. He is a senior. Good student. Good athlete. Very popular with the students and teachers. He'll shadow you your first few weeks to help you adjust. He'll even eat lunch with you. He'll make sure you have your books for your classes and such. Yes, you'll carry a book always here at Kennedy. It's why we're here. Derrick will report to me every other day on your progress. Or lack of progress. If I see you in my office, it'll be because Derrick reported you for something. In short, again, do the right thing."

Perfect, thought Jamal, now he has to worry about not only the adults, but also his own personal snitch spying on him and following him around all the time. He remained silent. This was certainly different from his Chicago school, and he was just in the first hours of his first day.

"Let me add one other thing, Jamal. I'm from Chicago. Spent a lot of time there. I know those same streets you come from. I grew up on the west side. Marshall High School. Bunch of guys I went to school with aren't around anymore. Dead. Doped up. Locked up. All of their own doing. I've been where you been and know from where you coming. You won't get any sympathy here. You will be judged solely on your own merit, meaning your behavior and grades are what will determine if you are successful here. No excuses will be accepted. You can't con a con-man, so don't even try. I'll come down hard on you, just like your grandfather. However, I can be your biggest supporter. You have a problem, bring it to me. You want to talk, come to me. The door's always open."

At this point, the office door opened, and big kid – Derrick, Jamal assumed – stuck his head in the office. "Hey, Mr. Griffith. Did you want to see me?"

"Yes, Derrick, come on in." Mr. Griffith got up from his seat and said, "This is Jamal Hayes. He's a new student from Chicago. This is his first day. I want you to get him acquainted with Kennedy High his first few weeks or so. Show him around, his classes, the layout of the land, so to speak. Jamal, this is Derrick Slater."

Slater extended his hand to the seated Jamal. Jamal stood and returned the handshake.

"Derrick here is captain of the football and wrestling team. He won the state in wrestling last year at 215 pounds," an obviously proud Griffith said.

"Nice to meet you Jamal. You play football?" asked Derrick.

"A little in the neighborhood."

"Well, maybe you can go out in the spring for football. We just finished our season. Went 7-3 this year, just missed the playoffs."

Mr. Griffith gave Derrick a piece of paper and said to Derrick, "This is Jamal's schedule. It's 4th period now. He should be in English with Ms. Caldwell. See that he gets there, but first show him around the building.

Give him the tour, so he'll know where to go tomorrow on his first full day."

"Yes sir," Derrick answered. "Come on Jamal."

With this, Mr. Griffith again offered his hand to Jamal and said, "Welcome to Kennedy High School, Jamal. It is good to have you with us. Good luck."

The meeting was then over, and Derrick led Jamal into the hallways of his new school and his first class.

As the two walked down the hallway, Jamal was taken by one thing: the halls were early empty and quiet, a stark difference from his school in Chicago. The halls there, it seemed, were louder, with many folks wandering at any point during the day.

Jamal's grandfather was correct: the vacation was over.

— Two —

Kennedy High School reminded Jamal of the Detroit airport he'd seen on the flight from Chicago (a flight to the south by way of a city north of Chicago?) – it was a long, horizontal two-story structure, its hallways stretching from one end of the school to the other. The building spanned most of the block it occupied. The office was located in the middle of the building, dividing the long hallways into two equal parts.

The school was built in the 1950s but went through a small renovation in the 1990s. The school's gymnasium was located on the north end of the building, while the auditorium anchored the south end.

Derrick Slater said little as he gave Jamal the tour, pointing out to Jamal which hallways and classrooms were for which students. Freshman students were on one floor, while sophomores were on another. The juniors and seniors shared a hallway, as the two classes' number did not equal the underclassmen's. Just like his Chicago school: the higher the grade, the lower number of students.

"This is the gym," Derrick told Jamal, as the two entered it. A P.E. class was in session, which meant students were playing basketball. Well, some students were playing, while others sat on the bleachers.

As they walked towards the rear of the gym, Jamal noticed the various banners on the walls: District Champions 1988, Region Champion 1980, District Champion 1986. Most of the blue banners were from the 1980s. Ancient history. At the rear of the gym there was a door that led to another area. "Wrestling and Fitness" the writing on it said. Derrick looked to the P.E. teacher – Jamal didn't catch his name – and motioned for him to come open the door. With the door opened, Derrick waved his arm like some game show host and said, "This is the wrestling room." The room was actually a smaller gymnasium that had been transformed into a practice room for the wrestling team. Nearly the entire floor was covered with blue mats. Small white circles were evenly placed across the mat. One end of the gym was set aside for weights and other exercise equipment. The other had several ropes hanging from the ceiling, pull-up bars and several large wooden steps.

"Where's the ring?" asked Jamal.

"What ring?" Jamal returned.

"For the wrestling. The ring to get in...."

"It's not that type of wrestling. We don't do the WWE stuff. We wrestle like they do in the Olympics. You know what I'm talking about?

"Yeah, sure." Jamal had no idea what Derrick meant, but he didn't want to appear stupid on his first day.

"A lot of schools in Memphis don't have wrestling, but we do. It is one of the sports we are real good at." He pointed to one wall that had many banners on it, most of them championship banners from this decade. There were some pictures on the wall also, but it was too far away to see whose photos they were. "Basketball here ain't that good. Football is okay every year. We finished 7-3 this past season. I play football to stay in shape for wrestling." Jamal could see he was in good shape. He looked just like the WWE wrestlers and MMA fighters, all buffed up.

"What's it about? How does wrestling work?" They were walking around the room. "Do you just pick 'em up and throw them down?"

"Sort of. Why don't you come out to practice this afternoon and see? Give it a try even. See if you like it. Coach Russo won't mind. He's always telling us to be on the lookout for guys to bring out to practice. We just started practice a couple of weeks back. There're ten or twelve freshmen on the team now. Our first home match is on Wednesday. Wrestling is sort of like fighting, except you got rules. I love it. Been doin' it since my ninth grade year. Gonna' defend my title again this year."

Derrick Slater was the Tennessee state champion at this weight class and wanted to go back and win the 215 title again his senior season.

"We start practice at 3:00 sharp. When school's done, come on down to the locker room. They're over there." He pointed to a door on one end of the room. "All you need is a t-shirt and gym shorts to practice. Coach won't let you just watch or go in school clothes. If you are in the room, you are on the mat."

"I'll have to call my grandfather to see if it's okay. I got some shorts with me."

"Call him on your cell."

"I don't have one."

"Well, you can call him on the office phone. You can do it before you go to your class."

Derrick then led Jamal back through the gym and into the school's hallway. Jamal might just give this wrestling stuff a try. Anything to avoid the workload his grandfather had most likely lined up for him.

• •

Lonny Hayes, at first, said no, but he eventually agreed to let Jamal stay after school, but only after speaking with the principal to see if Jamal was telling the truth. He found out that practice typically began at 3 PM and ended at 6:00. Mr. Hayes was also told the coach's name and where he could pick Jamal up at after practice. The man couldn't just say okay and be done with it. He had to know everything. Once again, his grandfather's words came back to him: "The vacation is over."

Jamal's history teacher had sat him in the front row. It was 6th Period, the last class of the day. Jamal felt as if everyone was staring at him. "The new guy." English class hadn't been that bad. The class had read a segment of *The Odyssey,* a story Jamal had somehow remembered from his Chicago school. While he "got" it, the story was still hard to read and believe. A big one-eyed, hairy monster called a Cyclops? Come on. For homework, the class was instructed to create their own monster for Odysseus to face in one of his adventures. Jamal made sure he noted the assignment in the "student planner" his grandfather had gotten him. He would want to see. Jamal thought a huge sea-monster of a sort would be good enough. He couldn't draw, but he'd write a description, one good enough to get a decent grade. Aim for the low trees, so to speak.

At 2:15, the bell rang, ending his first day – well, half day – at his new school. So far, so good. At least, he didn't get into a fight or any trouble. He didn't have a locker yet, so all of his books and materials were in his gym bag, which would have to double as a backpack for a while. He asked a teacher which way to the wresting room and headed that way.

He didn't know what to expect, but he sure knew it didn't have anything to with yard work or physical labor. It had to be better than what Lonny Hayes had in mind. Jamal hated hard work, manual labor and didn't want a day at school to be followed by a lot of sweating.

If only he knew.

— Three —

Coach Zane Russo appeared to be 40, but he looked like he could still line up and play linebacker like he did in his college years. He was 6'2" and weighed well over 200 pounds. It was obvious he still hit the weights, as his barrel chest and large biceps stretched the sleeves of his t-shirt.

With a blow of the whistle at promptly 3:00, Coach Russo had the team gather at his feet on the edge of the mats. Jamal took his place among the team members. There had to be over thirty-five wrestlers on the mat. There were small guys, medium guys (like himself) and big heavyweight-type guys.

Coach Russo brought the group to order.

"Settle down and listen up. First, the week ahead: practice today and tomorrow. Wednesday is our first home match. Gonna' get everyone matched up. Thursday and Friday, practice. Saturday, the freshmen and the JV go to St. Paul. Let you know the times on Friday. Of course, miss practice, and don't bother showing up on Saturday morning. Don't end your season before it begins. Show up."

Jamal would learn that Coach Russo had one rule: "Show up."

"Secondly, we got us new kid today. Jamal. He just moved to the area from Chicago. It's his first day ever on a wrestling mat. If you find yourself partnered with him, show him what we are doing, get him into it.

"Okay, let's go!" Coach Russo blew his whistle, and the team circled up around the edges of the huge mats. Four wrestlers were in the center of the human circle, one facing each direction. Each took a turn calling out a particular stretch and leading the group in it. There were stretches for the arms, the shoulders, the legs and the lower back. After ten minutes or so of stretching, the team began to do push-ups. Jamal followed the lead of those around him. There were regular push-ups, push-ups done on the knuckles and on the fingertips.

Coach Russo then took the lead. "Clap push-ups!" Coach would blow the whistle, and the team, in a push-up position, would push themselves up to clap their hands, resuming the starting position. That whistle must have been blown thirty times, meaning thirty of these push-ups. All the while, Coach Russo demanded: "Backs straight! Explode up!" Coach Russo paced the entire mat. "Front bridges!" he next ordered. Jamal was clueless, but he looked around and assumed the position: making a literal triangle with his body, his head and two feet serving as the base. With his hands at the lower part of his back, Jamal and the team worked their necks, rolling their heads frontwards and backward. Another whistle followed with the wrestlers hopping their feet over their heads, putting their bodies in the opposite position of where they started with a back bridge. Thirty seconds on the back were followed by a whistle, a hop and thirty seconds on the front, all the while keeping all the body's weight on the neck. Jamal never once got the hop-over either way. He simply assumed whatever position the team was in. After what seemed an eternity, or at least five minutes, Coach Russo again blew the whistle. "Move your feet!" Each wrestler was in a back bridge moving their feet in a circle around their heads. The point was to keep your neck in one place, while your body rotated around your neck. It was difficult and hurt. After a minute, Russo blew the whistle again. "Pair up and grab a circle!"

The wrestlers got a partner and each pair found one of the small white circles on the blue mat. There were eighteen circles on the two mats Jamal was paired up with a wrestler named Mark, a junior who weighed about the same as Jamal. He was about the same height as Jamal but looked to be much stronger. This is who I have to work out with, he thought. This guy will kill me.

"Let's start with our stance. Remember, butt down and head up." The whistle was blown, followed by the wrestlers chopping their feet, running in place. On the next whistle, the team froze into their stance. Jamal didn't know how to get a stance, but Mark helped him get into a square stance with his hands out in front of him. Another whistle, chopping feet, whistle, stance. This went on for nearly a minute. The stance felt awkward, but Mark told, "Don't worry, you'll get it."

"Levels!" the ever-roving Russo yelled, blowing his whistle. The wrestlers moved around each other, faking high and low with their hands, but never touching their partner. A wrestler had a lower level and higher level. It was important to be able to move and change your levels at the same time. Other drills would follow the level change: circles, hand fighting, stalking, sprawl, lunges, lifts, shots, sprawl-shots. While he took it all in, he was certain there was no way he would remember it all. There certainly a lot of movement involved in this stuff. When would he get to head-lock someone?

"Ropes," said Coach Russo. The entire team went to a wall near the coach's office to get one of the jump ropes hanging on it. Jamal went and got one. Wrestling was supposed to be for tough folks. What were the ropes for? Girls jumped rope.

All the wrestlers found their own space in the room, and on the toot of the whistle, began jumping their ropes. Jamal jumped fine for ten seconds or so before tripping in his rope. He couldn't seem to do more than ten seconds at a time, couldn't find the rhythm of those around him, who effortlessly jumped their ropes. Several wrestlers were even jumping big thick ropes that weighed four and five pounds, and they jumped them like boxing champs. Jamal couldn't navigate his fast rope; he'd hate to have one of those fat ropes. After what seemed an eternity (which was only two minutes), Coach Russo blew his whistle and said, "Twenty-five push-ups." Push-ups, again, thought Jamal. He did them. "Round two." Russo blew the whistle again. At the end of that period, he said, "Corkscrews." Jamal didn't have any idea what a corkscrew was, but he assumed a sit-up position like his teammates. On a whistle, one of the older wrestlers began the exercise: "One-two-three-One!" Each wrestler was taking his right elbow and touching it to his left knee, followed by his left elbow touching his right knee in sync with the leader's count. After twenty-five of these painful sit-ups, Jamal was the last one to his feet for round three of rope. In between each round push-ups were alternated with corkscrews. By the end of the sixth and last round, Jamal had done fifty more push-ups and fifty corkscrews to go with the crunches at the start of practice. Thirty minutes or so into his first practice, and he had already done nearly 100 push-ups and sit-ups, not to mention that neck torture. He hadn't done 100 push-ups in his entire life. The rope work had him sweating like crazy.

Coach Russo transitioned the team to the next phase of practice on the mat. It was series of drills like the front end of practice, except these involved a little more movement and contact. Coach would call out the drill, and the team would hit it. Jamal didn't know the movements, but he followed the lead of his partner Mark. Even with the help of Mark, Jamal was lost. Who knew wrestling could involve so much movement of the entire body?

As Coach Russo blew his whistle and watched his stop watch, he walked around and monitored the practice, stopping and correcting, as well as encouraging. Occasionally, profanity accompanied the encouragement – "Get your ass working!" He watched everything and everyone. His assistant was Coach Nelson, one of the school's football coaches. He was absent today, which would happen a lot, except for out of town trips. Coach Nelson was a wrestling coach in name only. He was good friends with Coach Russo and only helped out on days when there was a scheduling conflict. If the varsity and the JV teams had events at different places, Coach Nelson took the JV. He didn't help much in the day-to-day practices. However, Jayson Matthews, a former wrestler at Kennedy, was there to help. He had arrived a little late. He often came by to help Coach Russo, as did other former Kennedy wrestlers.

The whistle blew. "Take two!" Coach Russo stood with Jayson, while the entire wrestling team sprinted to the water fountain or the bathroom. Wrestlers took a sip of water and returned to the mat. Russo and Jayson stood talking in the middle of the mat. Moments later, Coach Russo began a countdown: "10-9-8…" Wrestlers hurried back to the mat. It seemed, by the sprinting, that you didn't want to be at the fountain when he got to"1."

The team seemed to know what was coming next, as they lined up at the door leading back into the school. Jamal took his place in the line, only to have Russo tell him to stay with Jayson and three other wrestlers. They were freshmen; Jamal knew them from one of his classes that day. Russo said to Jayson, "Eighteen minutes. Tighten them up."

The team followed Coach Russo into the main building, leaving behind the four wrestlers and Jayson.

Jayson reviewed some of the things that the team had done: stance, movement, balance. He demonstrated a double leg takedown and a counter to it. Jamal and the new guys would do it. Jayson told them they only needed to learn a few basics to be good: double, sprawl, half-nelson, and a stand. He would spend the next fifteen minutes going through these basic moves, showing them from the various positions—standing, top and bottom. "Keep it simple," he said. "You will learn all the fancier stuff as you go. Get these basics down, first." The small group continued to work under the guidance of Jayson. Jamal was feeling it. He was getting the few things Jayson had taught him.

The rest of the team was in the main building running the school's hallways. They returned and took their place on the mats. Coach Russo told everyone to get into groups of four, and to number off 1-4. Once assembled into the groups, Coach Russo said, "Takedowns. 1-2 and 3-4." Wrestler number one would battle number two and three would compete with number four. Coach Russo blew the whistle, and the wrestlers went at it, attempting to take their opponent down to the mat. Once a takedown was gotten, both wrestlers were back on their feet and at it again. Jamal's group included three freshmen. He was number two. He did well with number one, getting takedown after takedown. He only knew a double leg takedown, but he had gotten it down pretty well. A whistle blew. Coach Russo said, "1 and 3. 2 and 4." Partners were switched. Jamal had another opponent now, a kid a bit bigger than him. His double didn't work with him. Jamal shot at his legs only to be slammed down to the mat, and the kid getting behind him "Get your head up," Jayson told him. Jamal attacked again, with the same result: his head snapped down to the mat, the kid on top of him. "Don't just run in there. Fake at him. Set the thing up," Jayson told him. He demonstrated what he wanted. Jamal tried it. He moved in his stance, changing his level, faking at his partner. His partner reached at him, and Jamal quickly attacked his leg, moving under his reach, and taking him down. "That's how you do it," Jayson told him. "Now do it like that every time." The whistle blew, and Coach Russo ordered the team to the last rotation: 1-4 and 2-3. More takedowns followed.

The next whistle found the wrestlers on the mat, one in the up position and one in the down position. A whistle would blow, starting the action.

The wrestlers were to work until points were scored. Jamal didn't know how points were scored, so he just tried to throw his partner on his back or keep him from getting away from his grip. By the end of this phase, the entire team had worked some on their feet, some on the top and some on the bottom. Jamal was beat. He had no idea you could get so out of breath just wrestling.

The team was ordered next to get a partner and a circle. "From your feet to the mat," Coach Russo said. He was on Jamal's side of the mat and told him what this meant: "We start on our feet and we act like it is a real match. You just continue the action." Jamal had another partner now, one a little smaller than him. The whistle blew, and the wrestlers began their work. An orchestra of combat broke-out, as the various pairings went after each other. One takedown was followed by a reversal of some sort. Jamal took his opponent down, only to find him immediately standing up. Jamal didn't know what to do, so he let him go and took him down again. This pattern repeated three or four times until his opponent hit a reversal and Jamal found himself on bottom, the victim of a roll of some sort. He stood and tore free, only to have his opponent take him down right to his back in a bear hug. Since Jamal got put on his back, the two wrestlers were brought back to their feet by Jayson, where the entire cycle was repeated: takedown, escape, takedown, escape. Coach Russo blew his whistle and ordered the team to hit the mat: "Twenty-five push-ups." Some of the wrestlers groaned. It was the end of practice, but today the "regressive" phase would end it. You start at three minutes of live wrestling, followed by twenty-five push-ups. Then you wrestle live for 2:45 seconds, followed by twenty-five corkscrews or some other type of stomach exercise. Partners would be switched, and then 2:30 seconds of live wrestling ensued, to be followed by twenty push-ups of a different type (knuckles, claps). The idea was to wrestle live all the way down to where just fifteen seconds were in a period. By the end of a regressive phase, over twenty minutes of live wrestling had occurred, and the wrestlers had done over 75 push-ups and 75 reps on the stomach muscles, the "abs." Coming at the end of the day, it was taxing. It was designed that way.

Jamal's arms and legs felt like jell-o. He had never done three hours straight of anything other than sleep. His various partners in the regressive – all experienced wrestlers—dominated him thoroughly.

More groans followed the next whistle and directive from Coach Russo: "Shoot-and-leap!" An end of the day drill, it was designed to make the wrestlers push themselves when they were tired, while working their "shots." After three hours of his first practice, Jamal personified the word "tired."

Shoot-and-leap required a partner. One wrestler would stand in a good stance with his feet as wide as his shoulders. The other wrestler assumed a one-knee start stance in front of his partner's opened legs. On the whistle, he would shoot the legs of his partner and then leaping over the back of his partner, only to shoot through the legs again and leaping back over. The drill was done for time. The idle partner counted how many reps his partner got. One cycle – a shot and a leap – constituted one repetition. The idea was to get faster as you got more tired. It didn't happen for anyone this day.

Coach Russo started the drill with his whistle. He would tell the team when the clock was at thirty seconds, and then he would count down once the clock got to ten seconds. At the end of the first round, he would ask each pair of wrestlers how many reps were done. Today, one of the lighter wrestlers had gotten thirty reps. Jamal had barely gotten nineteen. The wrestlers would then swap positions, with the exhausted wrestler now doing the counting. If no wrestler in the second group got at least thirty reps, the entire group had to do it again.

When shoot-and-leap was done, Coach Russo signaled the end of the day. "Circle up and cool it down." The wrestlers got into the same circle they did to start the day with the same four guys in the center. On the whistle, the entire group broke out into twenty-five moderately fast jumping jacks, followed by leaping to the ground and ripping twenty-five push-ups (more push-ups), and followed still by twenty-five crunches. These reps were counted by the guys in the center of the circle. At the end of the crunches, the wrestlers were back on their feet with fifteen jumping jacks, push-ups and crunches. The last go-round was then of each, at which point, a huge sigh of relief was let out by most on the team.

Coach Russo was in the middle of the circle; Coach Russo echoed what he told the guys at the front end of practice. "Practice tomorrow, Match Wednesday. St. Paul on Saturday. Let's go weigh in." He left the mat and headed into his office, followed by the team coming together in the circle. . Derrick led the group. "Get it in. Hands in. Good job today. Let's do it again tomorrow. 1-2-3, Team!"

Everyone then went into the locker room. A scale was set up to weigh each wrestler. The line was long, with seniors in the front, juniors next, followed by the 10th graders. The freshmen were last. Bottom of the food chain. Coach Russo stood by the scale, checking each wrestler's weight. When Jamal stepped onto the scale, the red numbers on the scale raced and then settled at 154.2 pounds. Jamal had lost over five pounds during practice. A lot of sweating. Coach Russo noted the weight on his clipboard. "You can get down to 152 for the season." As he stepped off the scale, Coach Russo asked him, "What did you think?"

"This stuff is hard, but I liked it."

"Glad you gave it a try. If I see you tomorrow, great, if not, it was fun. You might want to stretch tonight before you go to bed. You're going to be sore tomorrow. Stretching can help you be less sore. See you tomorrow."

"Okay." Jamal left the office and went to get dressed. His grandfather would be waiting in the parking lot outside the gymnasium.

A few of the wrestlers lingered outside the gymnasium door, waiting for their rides. Derrick Slater saw him. "You did pretty well out there today for your first day. I was watching you. Keep with it. You got the stuff to be pretty good. We'll see you tomorrow."

"Thanks. I'll be here."

His grandfather was waiting in his truck. Jamal hopped in, and the two headed for home.

— Four —

In the time he'd been under his grandfather's roof, Jamal had walked on eggs. He didn't understand the great change in his grandfather. There was a time not so long ago that a trip to his grandfather's house was great, filled with fun and smiles: fishing, swimming, cookouts, and baseball games. There was no joy now; his grandfather always seemed mad, and that anger was seemingly aimed at Jamal. It was as if his own grandfather didn't even like him. The man never smiled, wearing a constant scowl, ordering Jamal around and making him work. What happened?

When told by his mother, Anna Hayes, that he was going to live with her dad, Jamal was excited. Easy street, he thought. This excitement turned to drudgery shortly after he arrived.

"Boy, go in there, put your stuff up and come in here and eat. Then get your school work done."

Even though it was his first day at his new school, Jamal knew he'd better have some homework of a sort, even if he had to fake it. His grandfather had told him he'd better have some books with him when he got home. "Yeah, I got to do something for English."

"Is that it?"

"Yeah –"

"Yeah?" There was no questioning the tone in his voce or the look on his face.

"Yes sir," Jamal said quickly, correcting himself. Jamal's grandfather insisted he address any adult, no matter their age, with "sir" or "ma'am." "I was only in school for half the day. I'll go to all my classes tomorrow."

"Alright. We'll eat, and then you get to that work."

Jamal went into his room – his mother's room when she was his age – and unloaded his gym bag. Wrestling practice was still on his mind. That stuff was hard, but he liked it. While his workout partners got the best of him in the live drills, they also pointed out any mistakes and showed him other moves. They'd demonstrate the move, and then let him do it. The guys made him feel welcome and encouraged him his first day. There was no "checking" or goofing off. Wrestling practice was strictly business from start to finish. Coach Russo didn't have to say a word; he just blew his whistle. The team leaders did the rest.

Going through that first practice oddly gave Jamal a sense of belonging. Though he didn't know anyone's name (except for Derrick), it was nonetheless like he had friends. Since coming to stay with grandfather, there had been little time for anything other the chores assigned to him by his grandfather. He had ventured little beyond the fence that surrounded his grandfather's house. The streets of "North Memphis," his new home, were a stranger to him, which was the opposite of his existence in "The Windy City." The "streets" were his virtual home and playground.

Of course, it was those mean streets that landed him in Memphis.

On Chicago's South Side, he spent more time on the streets than he did at home. Whether hanging out in the park, shooting hoops or talking up some girl, Jamal always had a reason to stay out rather than to be at home. "Home" was a (supposed) two-bedroom apartment, though it was more like a bedroom and half. Jamal's bedroom was more like a large closet instead of a full room. The Garland Homes apartment complex, a large conclave of two-story structures, replaced the "projects" that once occupied the land: three tall apartment structures with a huge parking lot. It reminded Jamal of the opening of the 1970s show "Good Times." The "Smith Towers" were each thirty-two-story buildings which were in a constant state of disrepair. If the cockroaches ever decided to leave, the buildings would have fallen to the ground.

The Garland Homes were just a few years old, but the vibe stayed the same. There were a lot of bums, crime and violence. It didn't take long before the gangs – Bloods, Crips, G-Ds – took over each block. The police were everywhere, but they had little effect on the area. How could they? They could only react. As soon as they ran someone to jail, two or three would be ready to take their place.

Anna, or so Jamal thought, had little time for him; at least, it seemed that way to Jamal. Frankly, Anna had little time for anything outside of her "problem," a habit she acquired in response to the stress of life as a single mom on the south side of Chicago. What started as a diversion from the daily aggravations of her good job at a downtown law firm caused her to lose that job, only to cause her to take two lower paying jobs to make ends meet, which in turn led to more stress and frustration prompting more and more "diversion," which caused Anna to lose those jobs, leaving her plenty of time for "diversion" and no time for the supposed stress and problems that necessitated the need for a diversion in the first place. As much as Jamal disliked the notion, his mother was a crack addict, a "crack head," and there was little he could do about it. So he did as he pleased – running the streets looking for acceptance and even love, two items that were once in abundance in his household.

The two had once been inseparable. Each Saturday was a day of adventure. As far back as Jamal could remember – excluding the last two years, of course – his mom had been his best friend. Some of his fondest memories happened on those Saturdays. Every Saturday, no matter the weather, Anna had something special for Jamal and her to do. Chicago has much to offer, and Jamal had seen and experienced much of it: museums, art galleries, professional sports events, ritzy shops on Michigan Avenue. Jamal loved the Museum of Science and Industry, as well as Wrigley Field. He'd been to the museum twice and attended just one Cubs game; maybe "love" was too strong a word. What he loved the most was spending time with his mom. He remembered being a little boy and beaming with pride as Anna held his hand as they walked down Michigan Avenue. His mom, he thought, was the prettiest woman in the world, and he loved to show her off on Saturdays.

At fifteen, he missed those days greatly. It was as if the moment he wasn't a cute "puppy" anymore, his mom had little time for him.

Jamal's father, one Marvin Worth, had baled on Anna and Jamal when Jamal was just a baby. Jamal had heard his father was a great high school athlete, one good enough to get a scholarship to college. While his athletic skills may have been great, his academic skills were not. He flunked out after one year of school. Jamal last heard he was doing twenty-five to life in an Illinois prison. He'd killed someone over a dice game. Great guy.

Jamal often wondered how his mom could get involved with a character like Marvin Worth.

Long story short. An extended Labor Day weekend by Anna and two college friends included dinner and drinks at a swanky downtown restaurant and bar. It was the start of their junior years at the University of Memphis. Anna was pre-law, while her friends were each working on an MBA. The weekend was supposed to be a last big blowout for the three before the fall semester truly kicked into gear, and they had to hit the books like crazy. That Friday evening changed Anna's life forever. She met Marvin Worth – Marvin "Worthless", as her parents called him—and the naïve and sheltered Anna never stood a chance against a hustler like Marvin. Anna didn't return to school; she moved to Chicago, much to the disdain of her parents. Jamal was born eight months later. While the young couple swore they'd make a go it as a family, it was only Anna who meant it. The responsibilities of family life were too much for Marvin. He bolted for the door after one month of fatherhood. The only "memory" Jamal had of the man was a photo of the young family taken at the hospital the day after Jamal was born.

Anna's long hours of work to take care of her son took its toll on her. The stress and worry broke her. While she was able to keep things together for some years, she eventually cracked. Or was it got into "crack?" Whatever the case, the last few years were a blur for Jamal. Mom wasn't home much, and when she was, she was usually out of it, passed out or sleeping on the couch. So he just hung out with his friends, his "boys" – Travis, Samuel, and Patrick. He told his mother they were friends from school, even though none of the three regularly attended school. Though none of the three were "officially" in a gang, they were close. The three often wondered aloud why Jamal bothered to fool with school. After awhile, Jamal did too, and his attendance and his mediocre grades all began to drop.

Petty crimes, shooting hookey and smoking a little weed began to replace the "Three Rs" in Jamal's world. With his mother barely able to stumble out of bed each day, he fended for himself. It was just a matter of time before real trouble found Jamal. *An idle mind is the devil's workshop.*

And it happened.

An auto-theft charge landed all four of the "boys" in jail and in front of a judge. Travis pulled-up in front of the Garland one day in a black jeep. It was his cousin's, he told them. "Don't worry," he implored. A joy-ride on Lakeshore Drive caught the attention of the police. They were busted.

The auto-theft charge got each a brief stay in the juvy-jail. A court hearing also saw the child protection services involved. Anna was in no shape to be in front of a judge or the social services folks. She was threatened with having Jamal taken away from her unless she could guarantee that

Jamal would be in school and have a suitable home. The only suitable home Anna had ever known was her childhood home, so she arranged for Jamal to be moved to the south and her father's home.

The court-appointed attorney told Anna that Jamal would probably get probation, since he was a first-timer. He was correct. The judge gave Jamal probation and community service. Anna, in a rare moment of sobriety, asked the judge if it would be okay to have Jamal moved to the south, away from Chicago. The judge agreed, and soon Jamal was scuttled off to Memphis and the home of Lonny Hayes.

The scene at O'Hare was emotional. Jamal didn't know where the airline ticket came from; it sort of appeared amidst all the turmoil. He'd later find out that his grandfather had paid for it. The tears flowed like rivers down both mother and son's faces. That last hug before he stepped on the place was more like a vise, gripping and refusing to let go: "Jamal, I love you so much, more than anything, more than life itself. I am doing this because I love you so much. I have to get some help. It won't be that long, and I'll get you back with me. I promise." She wiped the tears away. "Your grandfather loves you, and he'll take good care of you until I can get you back. Mama's gotta' do this not only for herself, but also for you. I'm messed up. Been messed up for some time. I ain't no good for either of us. I'm all messed up inside, and the doctor is going to fix it. I absolutely hate putting you on this plane, but it's the price I got to pay, so I can get us back right."

"Mama, I don't want to go. I want to stay and help you. I never been away from you." The tears were flowing. "I don't want to go."

"You have to go. Court said so. If you stayed, they might take you away from me for good. I'm gonna' work real hard at getting better. It might only be a month or so, but whatever it is, understand this ain't got nothing to do with you. You didn't do anything, and if you did, it's because of me you did it. It's my fault we got this mess, and I am the one that's got to clean it up." She wiped more tears away. "Now, you get on that plane. You be my little man. You be strong for both of us. Things will be fine soon. You'll see. This is a bump in the road, that's all. Now, you call me when you get to Daddy's. I don't go into the hospital for a few days. Call me whenever you feel like it."

Jamal hugged her again. How many hugs in a minute was the world record? What was the longest or strongest hug? He was sure he held all hug records now.

The last announcement was made for passengers to board. Anna had to force Jamal to let go. "Mama, I don't want to leave you," he said, "let me stay with you." Other passengers were staring. Jamal didn't care. "I don't want to leave!"

"I can't let you stay son. Now, you be the man of this family and get on that plane. Call me the minute you get off in Memphis."

Jamal finally let go of his mother, and with a face full of hurt, he walked to the attendant waiting by the gate to take his ticket. He waved a sad goodbye to Anna, and he disappeared into the Delta jet. "Seat 15-C." He hated 15-C, just as he hated Delta Airlines. Each took him away from his mother.

In a matter of weeks, Jamal felt this was a prison in itself, far worse than probation and washing police cars.

His grandfather's house, while old, was well kept. Located in North Memphis, a section of town just north of downtown Memphis, Jamal could see The Pyramid Arena from the house's backyard. A modest three-bedroom home, a fence surrounded the small and manicured lawn. The front porch – the "stoop" his grandfather used to call it – was a popular gathering place for summer evenings past. While the neighborhood was in decline, his grandfather's house stood out; it was the only domicile that appeared to be in a livable state. Many in the neighborhood had fled, but

Lonny refused to leave. The house was paid for, and it had suited him for thirty years. There was no reason to leave.

Jamal never knew his grandmother. She was killed in a car accident before he was born. However, there were reminders throughout the house of her: photos and other mementos. His grandfather had never remarried, preferring to live instead with the memories of his "Claire." He never mentioned her, but Jamal could tell he still missed her. He had seen his grandfather once in his room – "their" room – sitting on the bed, holding a photo of her and just staring at it.

"Get in here boy and eat." His grandfather was in the kitchen. The smells further invited Jamal to the table.

While always clean and neat, the entire house was old. All the furnishings had seen better years. Stuck in the 1970s, it seemed. The television was a huge box-type thing, while the telephone had a cord on it and set on a table. Lonny didn't own a cell phone and didn't want one. A computer? Not in this house. Jamal did manage to pack some his games from Chicago, but they would be the only items in this house purchased in this decade.

No fast food or junk food in his grandfather's home. If it wasn't for Subway or McDonalds, Jamal wouldn't have eaten in Chicago. Dinner was at 6 PM sharp in his grandfather's house—6:30 today, because of practice. Jamal was expected to be at the table come mealtime, especially on Sundays.

There was a small garden – dormant now – his grandfather worked all summer, providing all the vegetables the home would need year round. Every meal had some sort of produce, whether Jamal liked it or not. Jamal had a feeling the small garden would also be a source of work come the spring.

The two ate in silence. Black-eyed peas, sliced tomatoes and some leftover ham. Lonny broke the silence. "How'd it go in school?"

"It was okay. I only went to a couple of classes. The school's not as big as my school back home."

"I'm surprised you remember much of your schooling up there, seeing as you didn't go much."

Always finding something wrong, thought Jamal.

"What's this rasslin' stuff about? I ain't heard of this stuff, except on TV."

"It's not like that TV stuff at all. That's what I thought too. It's the kind of wrestling they do in the Olympics."

"What, just pick 'em up and throw 'em down?"

"Sort of, I guess. It seems there's a lot more to it. It was my first day, so I don't know much about it. It was real tough. A lot of push-ups and exercises and stuff. A lot of sweating."

"I let you go today because you ain't had much time to do anything since you got here, but I ain't sold on it yet. I'm gonna' get up there and talk to that coach and find out everything about it. Got to keep an eye on you."

"There's a lot of guys on the team. We stay in the practice room all the time. Coach Russo is the coach. He'd talk with you. Tell you all about it. I really liked it and would like to keep on doing it."

"You like it, huh?"

"Yes sir. It was hard, but I liked it. I've never done a sport in school. Always played in the neighborhood. Don't like basketball and ain't tall enough. I like this. It's one on one. Nobody out there but you. I like that. We got a match Wednesday, and coach said everyone would get a match. Said there was a tournament on Saturday."

"Wednesday. Where's it at?"

"At the school, he said. The tournament is at a school called St. Paul's. Coach said he'd get all the information to us on Thursday."

"What time is this thing Wednesday?"

“I don’t know exactly. We was told to get to gym after school.”

“I’m gonna’ talk to coach tomorrow; find out everything I want to know.” More eating. More silence. “So you really like that stuff?”

“Yes sir.”

“Okay, Eat up and get to that school work.”

“Yes sir.”

— Five —

Jamal awoke at 3:00 in the morning – or was he "awakened?" He was stiff all over. From his head to his toes, he ached. Even the slightest movement was bothersome. Needless to say, sleeping was difficult, with every twitch hurting. Flipping from his back to his side required great effort. Maybe he should have stretched like Coach Russo had told him to do.

The alarm clock rang at 6:00 AM, ending the fitful night Jamal had experienced. It took a moment to get out of bed. His normally spry and agile body moved in slow motion, the lactic acid causing his entire body to feel like one big wound. The hot water of the shower offered temporary relief, but its soothing effects ended the moment he stepped out of the shower.

Jamal walked slowly to class that day, feeling every bit three times his fifteen years.

Derrick Slater saw him during lunch. "Sore?" he asked.

"A little bit."

"Don't worry. It'll go away. Get to practice today. You'll see."

Jamal couldn't imagine another day like yesterday, but he nodded and began to dread the thought of the first push-up.

Jamal did his best to organize all that was thrown at him in his classes that day. Frankly, he couldn't remember the last time he sat through an entire day of the "Three Rs": History, algebra, English, biology, gym and art. He received four books, a new locker and a list of supplies needed for his classes. All the teachers seemed nice, and they each welcomed him to Kennedy and wished him luck. He was also informed of afternoon tutoring sessions, if he needed them.

At 2:15, the bell rang, ending his first full day at Kennedy. He went to his locker and ridded himself of the books he didn't need to take with him. He had some algebra homework and a little reading in English. If his "boys" in Chicago could see him now – actually taking two school books home. They'd laugh and make fun of him. True, but they didn't live with anyone like his grandfather. They'd do the same if they did.

When Jamal walked into the locker room, Coach Russo called him into his office. "How you feel today?" he asked.

"Real sore and stiff," answered Jamal.

"To be expected. Good to see you back. It's called, the soreness is, lactic acid. It's your muscles telling you you're pushing 'em, getting' 'em into shape. It'll start going away a little each day. Get some Ben-Gay or some other type of heat rub at the drug store. Put it all over you at night. It'll get to feelin' better."

"Yes sir."

"I got a call from your granddad today. Gonna' meet with him after practice."

"He said he was gonna' talk with you."

""We'll get to that later. You get dressed for practice."

Jamal went to get dressed with the rest of the team. At 3 PM sharp, Coach blew the whistle, which caused the team to circle up around him. "Another day. Where else would you rather be?" he loudly asked, not really expecting an answer. "You gotta' be a fanatic to be good at this sport –

first one here, last one to leave. I want plenty of company at the end of the day. All of you fanatics, the entire team being the last to leave." He paused and looked around at the team. "I spoke with the coach at Warren. Got everyone matched up tomorrow, even the new guys. So let's start thinking about tomorrow. We haven't lost a home match in three years. I don't want to lose one tomorrow." He paused again for emphasis. "Get in here right after school tomorrow, so we can set the room up. Weigh-in is at 4 PM, match at 5:00. Get your folks and friends to come see us. We could use the gate money."

Coach Russo then blew the whistle again, and the team circled up just as they had the previous day, repeating the stretching and exercise routine of Monday. "Stretch good, Get the soreness out," Coach Russo said as he walked around the circle of wrestlers.

The team went through the various stretching exercises it had the previous day. After ten minutes or so, he again blew the whistle and told the team to make three lines on one side of the mat. The team members lined up with seniors in the front when the first order came: "Lunges," ordered Russo, and the wrestlers began moving. Five at a time, the team members each took a huge step placing their opposite knee on ground before taking another huge step and placing the other knee on the ground. The lines literally "lunged" across the mat. Once down and back. Coach Russo then shouted the next order: "Drag your toes," and the three lines of wrestlers obliged, going to a knee and dragging the opposite foot's toes, alternating legs as they went. This was followed by the next call: "Shots." This was putting the lunges and the laces together, resulting in a "shot" a wrestler might take to attack and opponent's legs. The three wrestlers in front of each line then assumed their wrestling stances and then "shot" across the mat, "reaching" for an imaginary leg and "pulling" themselves across the mat. This drill was followed by the weirdest exercise Jamal had ever seen: partner hops.

Each wrestler was paired up with a wrestler of equal height and weight. One wrestler would stand facing the gymnasium's wall, his back toward the direction each pair would move as a group. The other wrestler stood on his head in front of his partner. The standing wrestler would grab his partner by the waist and pull him up to where each wrestler looked the inverse of the other: one standing with his feet on the ground, and the other with his feet in the air and hands facing the ground. Each wrestler grabbed his partner's belt line and held tight. On the whistle, partner "A" would go back towards his head, throwing his partner's feet toward the ground. When partner "B's" feet hit the ground, he would do the same: throw his partner's feet back over his head. If done correctly, the pair would look like a human slinky going across the mat. Most, however, did not. Few of the pairs could do two turns without falling to the ground. The drill required great strength, balance and body control. Each pair had to work together to get the move right and propel themselves across the mat. The seniors and juniors could do it, but the freshmen and sophomores struggled mightily. Needless to say, Jamal and his partner, another ninth grader, were in the struggling group. One would pull the other over, and the partner couldn't continue it, dropping the other often on his head. The two would have to start anew. "Keep at it Jamal. You're not gonna' get it right away, but it'll come in time." Coach Russo encouraged the new guys to keep up with the difficult and awkward (and funny looking) exercise. It seemed forever for Jamal and his partner to complete their laps on the mat.

More exercises were performed, each of them done while moving across the thirty-eight foot mat: shots, handsprings, rocking chairs, shoulder rolls, bear crawls, monkey crawls. In minutes, Jamal was sweating bullets again.

Coach Russo's whistle changed the drill: "Levels!" he shouted. The team transitioned to the same drills that had begun practice the previous day. Jamal was more familiar with these and didn't look so out of place.

Drilling with partners on the mat continued for another twenty minutes at a fast pace. One drill would be done for a segment thirty seconds or so, and then another would ensue, Coach Russo calling out each change with a toot of the whistle. The team seemed to know the routine, as most were already engaged in the drill before the end of Coach Russo's order. Coach Russo constantly reminded the team of keeping a good stance and drilling hard. "Push yourself!" he instructed.

Jumping rope, Jamal's dread, was next, and just like the day before, each "round" of rope was immediately followed by a type of exercise: either push-ups or corkscrews. Jamal hated the corkscrews. They had his stomach killing him last night. Today, a new stomach exercise was called: "V-ups!" The team members took their places on their backs. Coach Russo would blow his whistle and the entire team would bring their hands to their feet, their fingers touching their toes, their body forming a "V" shape. "One!" the team shouted. Another whistle followed with the team popping up to a "V." "Two!" they shouted. Twenty-five was the stopping point, followed by another round of rope. Six rounds of jump rope also meant an extra fifty push-ups and sit-ups. Of course, different push-ups were alternated, as was different sit-ups: clap push-ups, corkscrews, knuckle push-ups, V-ups, fingertip push-ups and crunches. Jamal hated the clap push-ups. He would add "V-ups" to the exercises he hated.

After jumping rope, Coach Russo called out, "Scrambles," and each wrestler paired up again, each pair taking one of the small practice circles. Jamal would learn a scramble involved placing each pair of wrestlers in odd positions and angles on the mat, and on the whistle, a fight for control would ensue. One scramble called for each pair to lie on their side on the mat, with each wrestler's head lined up with his partner's feet. On the whistle, each quickly sprang up, attacking the other wrestler, trying to get control, which meant getting behind the other wrestler, controlling his movement. There were eight or nine different scramble positions the team went through.

The day's two-minute water break followed the scrambles. Most of the team then went into the main building with Coach Russo to run, leaving behind Jayson with the few new guys he had taught the previous day. He then went through the protocol and scoring of an actual match. "If you take a man down, it's two points for you." He demonstrated, using Jamal as his practice dummy. "When you take him down, if he stands up and gets away from you, that is one point escape for him." He told Jamal to get on top of him in the referee's position. Jayson demonstrated some type of roll and said, "If you're on bottom, and you reverse your opponent, it's two points for a reversal." Jayson last demonstrated how to get an opponent on his back, using a half-nelson. "The half is the most basic of moves, but it works. When you get your opponent on his back" – he then turned Jamal from his stomach to his back – "it is a two or three point nearfall for you. Just depends on how long you hold him on his back. Of course, if you squeeze him tight, you'll pin him. If you squeeze him real tight, and he hollers, that is a four-point nearfall. Don't happen much, but Coach Russo really likes those." Seeing the new guys' confusion, Jayson added, "Don't sweat all this new stuff and scoring. The referee will tell you where to go. Just go hard. Bounce 'em on their head like Coach Russo says, and you'll do fine. Look to Coach Russo, and he'll guide you and tell you what to do."

The rest of the team returned to the gym, and the live wrestling began. For the next hour and a half, each of the wrestlers worked hard, going after his partner like he was an opponent from another school. Occasionally, someone would complain of being hurt, prompting little or no response from Coach Russo. If he said anything, it was typically something like, "Roll off the mat. Don't have time for that now." The injured party usually rejoined the group instantly.

Jamal was covered in sweat when the final whistle of the day sounded. He'd held his own during the live sessions, getting the better of the various partners he'd had that day. Only the upperclassmen could handle him easily, and even they had to work at it. One senior named Danny had even told him he was going to be pretty good, "if he stuck with it." Jamal didn't really know what he was doing, but he was throwing folks around a bit and he wasn't on his back, so he figured he was doing something right.

Coach Russo was standing on one end of the practice gym, where the weights were located. "Line it up. Time to get the reps in," he said, eliciting a groan from the wrestlers. The team nonetheless moved to various stations in the weight area. Eight stations were set-up, including three on the mat. A 45 pound weight-lifting bar had been taken from one of the bench press benches and was lying in one of the practice circles. In the next circle was a volleyball and in the next a 45 pound weight-lifting plate. Each wrestler would spend a minute at each station and "rep out," meaning they'd do as many as they could do. "Start on the first whistle and stop on the second," said Coach Russo. A whistle would start and end each segment, and then the wrestlers would move to the next station. Jamal discerned that "the reps" weren't very popular with the team, especially coming as they did at the end of practice when everyone was already beat. Coach Russo met the groans with, "Doing this when you already spent is the point. I won't have any of my guys run out of gas in the third period. We make the other guy get tired."

Jamal's first station was the "plate hop," a station where the wrestler grabbed a 45 pound weight plate and held it with both hands at his waist. On the whistle, the wrestler hopped onto a wooden box-step that was a foot and half high. "Both feet on and both feet off," Coach Russo instructed. Jayson would count how many "reps" Jamal got. If one foot landed on the floor instead of two, that rep didn't count. Jamal barely got fifteen reps with the plate. His thighs and knees ached by number ten. The last five were very difficult.

The "hop-cleans" were next for Jamal. If he thought there'd be a break, an easy exercise, he was wrong. The hop-cleans were harder than the plate hops. The exercise started with the wrestler on his knees with a 45-pound bar on his thighs. On the whistle, he would perform one clean, bringing the bar to his chest and hopping to his feet. It was all done in one motion and involved, it seemed every muscle. Doing the reps in fast succession also required a lot of wind. At the end of the minute period, Jamal was out of breath, his legs and knees once again aching. He had done only ten. The hop-cleans involved technique, a technique he didn't have. "Keep doing it. You'll get it," someone told him. Who knew 45 pounds could become so heavy?

The other exercises – squats with a 45 pound plate, windshield wipers with a 35 pound plate, lunges with a 25 pound plate, alternating ball push-ups, and pull-ups – were equally difficult. None, however, were as tough for Jamal as the last one: the rope climb. A thick rope hung from the roof in one corner of the gym. Coach Russo had it pulled up during most of practice, so Jamal hadn't even noticed it. On the whistle, the wrestler was to climb the rope to a point twenty feet up and then slowly climb back down. There was no sliding down the rope. You did it from whistle to whistle – up the rope and down. Slowly. Of course, "slowly" was all Jamal could do. He didn't even get to the top once, losing his grip each time he would get ten feet or so up the rope. His muscles were sapped. The junior and senior members of the team made it look easy, climbing the rope like monkeys. Each of the freshmen and sophomores struggled to get halfway up the rope.

Once the team – all thirty-five members – had completed each of the eight stations, Coach Russo gathered the team on the edge of the mat. It was nearing 6:30. "Ran a bit over today," he said. "Had to. Big night tomorrow. Weigh-ins are at 4 PM. Match at 5 PM. I've spoken to the other team's coach. Everyone will be matched up. After school, get in here, so we can set up the room for the match. Any questions?" There were none. "Okay, let's go check the weight."

The team again circled up, this time in a big circle, each hip to hip, all heads facing the middle. Derrick Slater took the lead, ending the day. "First home match tomorrow night. We haven't lost at home in a long time. It ain't gonna' happen tomorrow." At this point, he started to smack the mat with both hands, slowly at first and then faster. The rest of the team joined in, creating a loud clapping symphony that echoed throughout the gym. After a minute or so, Derrick screamed, "One-two-three," prompting the team shout "Kennedy!" and "Wrestling!" This was followed by two loud thuds, the team pounding the mat with their hands for emphasis. The entire group then headed to the locker room, just like the previous day, to check their weight.

Lonny Hayes's arrival had escaped the notice of Jamal. He was sitting on the first row of seats in the bleachers. Jamal walked towards him. Noticing the soaked t-shirt, Mr. Hayes said, "Looks like they got you working in here."

"Yes sir."

"That's a good thing. I'm here to talk to coach."

"He's in the locker room in his office."

"I'll wait for him out here."

"Okay, I'll tell him you are here."

Jamal, once again, was one of the last to weigh-in. *Freshmen at the rear.*

He stepped on the scale. "152.0 pounds," noted Coach Russo. "Told you we'd get you down to your weight. I know my business."

Jamal was amazed. He'd dropped almost seven pounds in just two days. This stuff really burns off the weight, he thought.

"My grandfather is here. He'd like to talk with you. He's in the practice room."

"Great. Get dressed and go get him. Tell him to come into my office."

"Yes sir."

Jamal retrieved his grandfather, escorting him from the practice gym and into the locker room. Coach Russo was waiting at his office door, his hand extended. "Mr. Hayes, is it? Good to meet you."

"You too, Coach Russo."

"Jamal, we're going into the office for a minute. You can wait here or out in the gym with the rest of the guys."

Jamal wandered to the gym and waited in a chair by the door for his grandfather. His teammates had all left already.

Mr. Hayes didn't waste any time. "Coach, I got me some questions about this wrestling. Jamal moved in with me from Chicago. He had some trouble up there. The wrong crowd and stuff. I promised to keep an eye on the boy, keep him from doin' the same thing here. I don't know about this wrestling stuff –"

Coach Russo interrupted him. "I'll answer any questions you have. We've only had Jamal for two days, but he's got the stuff. I've seen it, and he's got it. A ton of potential in Jamal. And we can always use another good wrestler."

"How often do you practice? Do you have a schedule? When does this season end?" asked Mr. Hayes.

"The answer to the practice question is simple: everyday from 3-6 PM. Even on match days, we keep it the same. Less to remember for the guys. It also helps parents to know where their boys will be.

"Yes, I have a schedule." He took one off his desk and gave it to Jamal's grandfather. "This is the schedule for every level. Jamal is a freshman, so his schedule includes the varsity dates, as well as all freshman dates. As far as the season goes, it runs from November to February. The freshmen will most likely be done by the last week of January. The Freshman City Championships are then. We sometimes keep some freshmen – just the good ones – out until the end of the season."

"How 'bout schooling. This seems like a lot of time involved. When do the kids study?"

"Good question. We're sort of proud of our Kennedy wrestlers. Since I've been here with the program – I started it twelve years ago – the wrestling team has a 92% graduation rate and nearly a 100% promotion rate. In the practice room, there's a table and some chairs by the locker room door. If a wrestler is struggling with a class or has a test or big assignment due, that table is our study hall. They can get the lessons done and still practice when they're done. I can make sure they get both done. I tell the guys to take advantage of it, that they can still get to practice after their studying. If it turns into an everyday thing, then I get rid of them. If they have to go to tutoring or study here every day, then what are they doing in class during the school day? And what is homework if they are doing it here? If they are at tutoring or studying here every day, then wrestling may not be for them because it is keeping them from doing their best in their classes. Does any of this answer your questions?"

"Yeah, it sure does. Seems like the boy won't have time to think for himself, which is good in my book. All he'd do is get into some foolishness he ain't got no business fooling with." He paused. "The boy seems to like it. I want him to do well in school, as well as make some friends. Good friends, not those hoodlums I see in the streets every day. These boys seem like good kids, the kind I want Jamal to be with."

Coach Russo was nodding his head. "He's in the right place, Mr. Hayes. I got the best kids in the school on this team. They pass their classes, and they behave. I don't sweat fools. Of course, the sport itself does not lend itself to foolish people. It usually runs 'em off the first day. The wanna-be-thugs aren't going to do all this work. The wrestlers are good kids. They're proud of what we've managed to do here at Kennedy with this wrestling team. Jamal is a perfect fit. He works hard, and he seems to get along well with the guys. He's also one tough customer. I think he's going to be pretty good."

"The boy ain't never showed much interest in sports. He played football and basketball in his old neighborhood, but that's about it. This wrestling stuff kinda' caught me by surprise. He's never been in any organized sport."

"Wrestling appeals to a certain type kid. It ain't for everyone, but for those it gets, the sport becomes addictive. Much like the other combat sports. Boxing, karate, judo, the new MMA stuff."

"In my younger days, I did me some boxing. Golden Gloves and all. Fought some in the army too."

"Then you know how difficult it was – the workouts and all. In football, you can hide. You can't in wrestling or boxing. It's one on one. You can't hide in a ring or on the mat. I've found that wrestling builds upon whatever the character the kid has. Good character will be increased; low character will be exposed. The bad kids don't last; they quit. This sport runs 'em off. Wrestling has worked very well for this neighborhood. Many of my guys could have been the biggest thug in North Memphis, but wrestling saved them, gave them a bit of pride. Real self-esteem. Our principal – you did meet him? – says wrestling is the perfect sport for this area. And he's right. Bunch of young toughs around here. They like to fight. Wrestling ain't nothing but a fight with rules. They are no different than their classmates. They see all the negative in the area, the drugs, the gangs, the senseless violence, but they have turned away from it. They found something they like, and they go after it with a passion. Next thing you know, it is four years later, and they walk out of here a high school graduate, a real accomplishment in this area. Some of them even go onto wrestle in college.

But they all, and I mean all, go onto productive things after they leave here. As I said, this sport has been good for the kids at Kennedy." Another pause. "I apologize for the soap-box or the evangelizing, but I am real proud of what we've done here. Do you have any other questions?"

"No sir. I think Jamal is in the right place. I think it's a good thing you got here coach. These boys, many of 'em ain't got a dad at home. What you are doing is God's work. You're taking the daddy's place for many of 'em." Mr. Hayes was about to walk out when he stopped. "I do have to ask you something else. Does the boy need anything for wrestling? Any type of gear or outfit or equipment?"

"He could use some shoes. You can get them online or at any local store. Tomorrow night is our first home match of the year. I'll let him borrow some shoes. I keep extra pairs. When the guys graduate, they leave me their shoes. It helps with some of the boys whose folks can't afford any. I bet I got two dozen or so in my office. He'll also need a physical. I have a doctor coming tomorrow afternoon to do some for some new guys. It'll cost ten bucks. I can get you the forms for it now. The doctor will be here at 3:00, right before the weigh-in."

"I can have that for him. Let him use some shoes. I don't know about that online stuff, so I will just send some money with him, and you can order them for him. Anything else he needs, just let me know, and I will get it for him. I'd also like a weekly schedule sent to me on Mondays just so I can know what he's doing. I run the garage over at Empire Trucking. It ain't too far from here. Just call me with any problems."

"I don't think we'll have any with Jamal. If he just shows up everyday, he'll do fine. I will let you if he skips out on me."

"Good. I better get him home. I thank you coach for finding some time for me. I feel much better about things now. I'm gonna' get behind this thing and let Jamal do it."

"You're gonna' be here tomorrow, aren't you, Mr. Hayes?" asked Coach Russo. "It's our first match of the year, and I have Jamal matched up."

Mr. Hayes looked a bit confused. "So soon? Is he ready for that? He ain't been out but two days."

"It's just an exhibition against another first year kid. He'll do fine. If he wins, great. If he doesn't, no big deal. It's an exhibition. It'll be great to get his some experience."

"What time?"

"We'll start at 5 PM sharp. It'll be in this gym. It's our first match of the year. I'm hoping for a good turnout."

"Count me here. I don't know the first thing of what I'll be seeing, but I'm gonna' make a point of being here."

"Good, Mr. Hayes, see you then." Coach Russo shook hands with Lonny Hayes and went back into his office.

Jamal was waiting outside for his grandfather. The two jumped into the truck and were off for home. The previous night's routine was repeated: put away dirty clothes, study, eat, pack gym bag for tomorrow, bed.

As sleep began to overtake Jamal, he saw it was just 9:15. In Chicago, he'd never be in bed this early unless he was sick or something. Life with "Pop" was almost boring, just school and sleep. But it wasn't too bad; it was a good boring.

With two or three turns in the bed, coupled with an adjustment or two of the pillow, Jamal was off to sleep, his last thought being that some kid somewhere in Memphis was going to try to choke him out tomorrow night. It was a thought that would interrupt his sleep several times that night.

— SIX —

A sense of both excitement and dread followed Jamal around all day at school. He was excited about his first match, even though it was just an exhibition. He planned on picking his opponent up and putting him on his back. If that boy tried to get his legs, he'd hit him with a vicious crossface and take him down. Jamal had his match already worked out in his head. He was ready for whatever would happen. He would be the aggressor though; that is what coach said: "Be aggressive. *Always be aggressive.*"

Of course, there was the flip side to his eagerness – doubt and the fear that came with it. He might be the one to get bounced on his head. Somewhere in the city, a kid, probably the same age as Jamal, was planning to do some bad things to Jamal. Jamal might have to endure the crossface. Like an elementary school kid, who hated the end of the school day because a bully waited for him in the school yard, Jamal found himself with a bit of angst too. Someone was planning oh whipping his butt that night. *Just be aggressive* was foremost in his mind most of the day.

After school, Jamal gathered his stuff and headed to the practice gym. Some of the team had already gathered there, while others drifted into the gym in intervals. Several of the team members were already at work preparing the small gym for the evening's match. They had moved one of the huge mats to the side, leaving just one of the mats in the center of the gym. It was flipped over onto its competition side. A wide broom and two mops and buckets were nearby. Jamal jumped in and helped, doing whatever the older guys told him to do.

In minutes, Coach Russo called for the wrestlers who needed physicals. The doctor had arrived. Coach Russo had the doctor in his office, where he would do the physicals. There were six wrestlers who needed physicals. Jamal took his place in the line and waited. It took about twenty minutes before Dr. Wu, an Asian man who spoke little English, had finished with the guys in front of Jamal. It was his turn. Jamal hated doctors and hospitals. He associated both with shots, which he really hated. The mere thought of a needle gave him the creeps. "You ain't gonna' give me a shot, are you?" Jamal asked.

"Not unless you want one," answered Coach Russo.

"I was asking the doctor, coach."

"Well, he don't talk much. His English is a bit rough. Anyway, I don't have to be a doctor to answer that question. It's just a physical. They don't give shots for a physical. Just gonna' take your blood pressure and listen to your heart. Weigh you and see how tall you are. Just hope he doesn't have a rubber glove with him, Jamal."

"Why? What do you mean?" Jamal asked, a serious look on his face.

"Oh nothing." Coach Russo looked over at the doctor and asked, "You don't need your glove for this one, do you?"

The doctor had a confused look on his face, as if he had trouble understanding the coach's question. "Glove?"

"You know, for the butt thing, the rectal exam?"

Jamal's eyes got wide at the mention of the word "butt" and even larger at the word "rectal."

"Don't worry, Jamal, it will be the last thing he does, and you'll still be able to wrestle tonight. Maybe."

"Coach, I don't know if I want to do this."

"It'll be fine, don't worry. It doesn't hurt *that* much. Besides you'll be facing the opposite direction, and I will be helping hold you down. It'll be okay." At this point, Coach Russo winked at Dr. Wu and turned his head. Jamal could see he was holding back a laugh.

"You're just messin' with me, ain't you," said Jamal. He was relieved, a little relieved.

"Just a little. A physical ain't nothing to worry about at your age. Now, my age is another story."

The exam went well. Jamal passed it easily, as did the other five wrestlers. All six went into the gym to help with the set-up for the night's match. There was little work left to be done, outside of mopping, which all freshmen were told is "freshmen, grunt work." A single blue mat was in the center of the gym, taking up most of the center of the basketball court. Fourteen chairs were lined up one each side of the mat. Two had been set in two corners of the mat. Coaching chairs, Jamal assumed. The word K-E-N-E-D-Y was spelled down one side of the mat in large white block letters trimmed in red. A white circle was in the middle with a white outer circle. A small rectangle was in the center of the center circle. One side had a red line on it, while the other had a green line on it.

With an hour to go before the start of the weigh-in, Coach Russo gathered all the freshmen and other newer wrestlers on the mat. "We've gone over this before, but let's review how things will go tonight. Jamal, this is your first match, so we'll show what you can expect." He then had two upperclassmen help to demonstrate. "You'll start by going to the head scorer's table and report to the scorekeeper. The referee will there to make sure everyone is who they're supposed to be, and then he'll bring the two of you out to the center of the mat to the small rectangle you see here."

He pointed to the small rectangle in the center of the mat. "You'll get on the green line because it is the line on our side of the mat. Those chairs are where we will sit. Green is always the home color. Your opponent, of course, will be on the red line just across from you. The referee will tell each of you to take your place. You will immediately get into your stance." The two upperclassmen assumed a wrestler's stance. "The referee will tell each of you to shake hands, and then he'll blow his whistle, signaling the start of the match." Coach Russo blew his whistle, and the two upperclassmen acted as if they were wrestling.

After blowing his whistle again, Coach Russo continued with his lesson for Jamal and the new guys: "At the end of the first two minute period, the referee will bring you two back to the center. He will check with the head table to see who has choice. If it is our choice, look to me. I will tell you to choose 'down.'" He then pointed his finger in a downward direction. "Do this to the referee. He will tell the head table you chose down, and then he'll set you down in your position. The referee will ask if you are ready, and then he'll tell your opponent to take his place on top. He will set each of you, and then blow his whistle again. If you don't see me or forget to look, don't ever forget to choose down. There are more scoring opportunities when you are down. We will always choose down. Got it?" He waited for Jamal to nod okay. "When that whistle blows, you stand up and tear free from your opponent. Standing up is probably the only thing you know on bottom, and that's fine. If he throws you down, stand up again right away. Keep moving when you're on bottom. Got it?" Jamal nodded. "When the second period ends, the referee will bring you both back to the center and repeat what he did before, except this time he will ask your opponent his choice – 'Top, bottom or neutral.' He'll then line you up again and restart the action. Of course, if you pin the kid in the first period, we don't have to worry with all this. Pinning your opponent gives us six team points. You're wrestling an exhibition tonight, so there will be no team score, but still try to pin the kid. With only two days work, I don't know if you got the wind to go longer than the first period." He paused. "Any questions?"

Jamal, of course, had many questions, but he didn't ask any.

"Don't worry guys, you'll be fine. Win or lose, if you do your best and go as hard as you can, that's all you can do or I can ask of you. I'll never get on your ass as long as you're going hard and being aggressive. I will get onto you if you quit or dog it out there. Once that whistle blows, we at Kennedy only know one speed – full speed. Give me 110%, and we'll be fine. Remember, no matter the score, as long as you are standing, you got a chance."

About this time, the Warren team showed up, and they went into the locker room to check their weights. Coach Russo must have known the Warren coach because they had a friendly chat when the Warren team entered the locker room.

The referee soon arrived, and both teams weighed in for the match. The freshmen and JV wrestlers weighed after the two varsity teams did. Jamal weighed in at 154.5 pounds. Two and half pounds over yesterday. No match for me, Jamal thought.

The two coaches went into Coach Russo's office and stayed in there for ten minutes or so. When the two exited the office, Coach Russo told the team to get seated and to listen up. "We're good on the varsity lineup. Everyone made weight. We're all over the place with the freshmen. Coach and I had to rework some of the matches. Jamal, you got to bump up to 171 pounds because you were overweight. Coach didn't have a 160-pounder, so I had to pair you with a bigger kid. Don't worry, he only weighs 162 pounds. He didn't make 160, so you'll do fine."

Uniforms – "singlets" – were handed out by Jayson. Jamal was a bit surprised. Though he didn't know what a wrestling uniform looked like, he was not expecting something so clinging and tight. The Kennedy singlet was blue with a white panel down each side. A white block “K” was on its chest – sort of like the “S” on Superman’s chest. It was a shiny material – Lycra he would discover – and it was very tight. Every curve in his body was display for all to see. Jamal, like most boys his age, preferred his clothing to be loose and even baggy. This tight singlet would be almost like wearing nothing. Everyone would stare at him and laugh. But everyone else on the team would be wearing the same thing, so, Jamal surmised, they would be laughing at them too.

Jamal’s thoughts were interrupted by Coach Russo. “Jamal, here!” He tossed a pair of black wrestling shoes in his direction. “You can use these until you get some of your own. They’re a size 10. I bet they’ll fit.”

“Thanks, coach,” said Jamal.

“I always keep extra pairs of shoes, just in case anyone needs a pair. Your granddad has already said he’d get you some. Use these until then.”

“Yes sir.”

Jamal put on his singlet. Self-conscious didn’t begin to describe how he felt. The material was cool to his body, and in the drafty locker room, he felt downright cold. He hurriedly put on his shoes. A little big, he thought, but they’ll do. He then got into his hoody sweatshirt and gym shorts he had been told to bring by Coach Russo.

Ten minutes passed before Coach Russo got everyone’s attention. “Everyone up. Gather ‘round.” The team assembled on the locker benches and the floor outside his office. “First home match. Decent crowd outside. Let’s give ‘em a good show. It’s early in the season, but you never get a second chance at a good start. This is our place, and I don’t like to lose at home. Go hard, and don’t stop. Okay, circle it Derrick, and let’s get ready to go.”

The team circled around Derrick, the team captain and defending state champion at 215 pounds. He said a few encouraging words, and then led the team in The Lord’s Prayer.

Coach Russo was by the locker room door. When the team broke up after the prayer, he said, "Line it up. Captains in front, followed by the lightest to the heaviest. Ne guys, just jump in at your weight class."

The team lined up at the door. Derrick yelled, "Get it up!" Everyone began clapping their hands. Derrick hit the locker room door, opening it and leading the team out of the locker room and into the gym. Once in the gym, he led them in a light jog around the entirety of the gym before heading onto the mat, where he continued to circle until everyone was on the mat. A good sized crowd was in the stand and cheered as they circled up on the mat.

The team went through various stretches and exercises on the mat. Nothing like they did at practice, but sort of light warm-up stuff. After stretching, each wrestler paired off with another wrestler his own size, and the team drilled various moves, each wrestler cooperating with the other, letting him get the move. Derrick called out the moves to practice: single, double, sprawl, stand, sit-out, switch. He lost Jamal on the switch; he didn't know what that move was. After five or six minutes, Derrick called everyone into the middle of the circle, much like they ended each day at practice: on their bellies, all heads into the center of the mat. Derrick told the team in a low voice: "Let them hear us." The team slapped the mat, picking up speed with each second, before Derrick yelled, "1-1-3!," which was followed by the team smacking the mat twice, screaming "Kennedy," with two loud thuds on the mat to follow.

The team took their place on the chairs on Kennedy's side of the mat. As only fourteen chairs were set up, the fourteen starters got a seat. Behind the row of chairs was a small mat, as well as some jump ropes. Coach Russo had a chair to himself. Jayson sat next to him. He soon yelled, "Captains out!" Derrick and Andre Merrick, the team's star 130 pound wrestler, made their way to the center of the mat, where the Warren captains waited with the referee. The wrestlers shook hands and listened to the referee. The ref tossed a disc in the air, much like the referees do with a coin toss at a football game. Derrick said something to the referee, and he and Andre jogged back to the Kennedy side of the mat. "We got odd, Coach Russo, and we start at 130 pounds."

Coach Russo gathered the team around for one last word. He echoed what he had said in the locker room, adding, "Varsity, you got the seats first, then the new guys. JV, go sit on the bleachers until this match is over, and then you come on over."

The Kennedy 130 pound wrestler, Andre, ran to the scorer's table and checked in before running to the center of the mat. The referee checked with the scorer's table and time keeper to see if they were ready, and he then told the two wrestlers to shake hands. The whistle blew, starting the first wrestling match Jamal had ever seen, outside of the WWE, of course.

After a few matches, it was obvious, even to Jamal, that the Warren team was not as good as Kennedy, not by a long shot. Andre attacked his opponent on the first whistle, feinting with his left hand, and attacking both legs and lifting his opponent in the air. He then gently laid his opponent on his back and pinned him. It took all of :23 seconds. Many of the matches ended quickly. Jamal took it all in, trying to keep his game plan on his mind, while trying to pick up something else he could add to it. The varsity team's match ended in just under an hour. The final score was 68-9. How this score came to be was a complete mystery to Jamal, but it appeared to be a rout. Either Warren was not a very good team, or Kennedy was very good.

"New guys, take the bench," Coach Russo ordered. He then circled them up and spoke: "The varsity did a great job. Now it's your turn. We start at 135 pounds. "Karl" – the freshman at 135 pounds – "get loose. Everyone, when there are two matches ahead of you, start warming up. I'll let you know."

The freshmen and JV took the bench, and Karl began warming up. Jamal would be the fifth match to go. Suddenly, the nerves that had bothered him all day returned. Sweat returned to his palms. Where'd this come from? While he'd been nervous all day, he was very nervous now. Doubt crept in to accompany the nerves. He'd only had two days of practice. How could he possibly be ready to compete in an actual match? He didn't' belong here, at least, not yet.

Jamal tried to watch the other freshmen matches ahead of his, but all he could think of was his own. He saw his opponent across the mat. He was a big kid, one who was taller and bigger than Jamal. He probably had been out for wrestling the entire season and not just two days. The kid had to be stronger than Jamal. He looked like he was in the 11th grade and not the 9th. This kid had to know more about wrestling than Jamal did. *What have I gotten myself into?*

In no time, Jamal heard his name called to go to the mat. Coach Russo adjusted Jamal's headgear and calmly told, "Just be aggressive and do your best. Don't think too much, just throw him around like you're in your front yard. It's an exhibition. Have some fun. Look to me whenever the ref is talking to you, and I'll tell you what to do. You're gonna' do fine, believe me."

He was so nervous. His legs were shaking, and he just knew everyone in the gym could see them shake. He checked in at the head table and went to the circle and assumed his stance. *Don't let anyone see my legs shaking.* His opponent was much taller than he was. The referee told them to shake hands, and the whistle blew.

All the plans Jamal had strategically constructed disappeared the moment his opponent snapped his head down; survival instincts took over. As the kid maneuvered Jamal around the mat, all the stuff Jamal learned in practice was forgotten. Where was the double? Where was the bear-hug? In the practice room, that's where.

Jamal broke free from his Warren foe. He began to move in small circles. *This is familiar.* Move, circle, feint, level change. *It was starting to come to him now.* The Warren wrestler smacked Jamal upside his head gear, and then he did it again. *This ain't boxing.* Jamal moved left, then right. He feinted with his left hand and rushed the kid as he reached for him. Grabbing him in a bear-hug, Jamal squeezed. He locked his hands around his opponent's back and leaned into him, squeezing as hard as he could. "Trip him as you lean into him!" yelled someone from the bench. And Jamal did. His opponent went straight to his back and Jamal fell on top of him and tried to hold him down. The referee was signaling the count. Jamal couldn't get a good grip. It was like trying to hold a fish out of water, hard to get a grip. Jamal did everything, except the correct thing, to hold his opponent down and turn him onto his back. He pulled his arm, pressing down on his shoulder. No good. The Warren wrestler got free and stood up. The referee signaled "1 point escape." The two adversaries were back on their feet in the center of the mat. Jamal looked at the scoreboard. Someone was winning 4-1. *Jamal didn't know it was he who was winning.* Coach Russo held up two fingers. Jamal didn't have a clue. He'd later learn that it meant a double-leg takedown.

Moving around his opponent, Jamal feinted with his left hand again – heck, it worked the first time. A second feint of his right hand saw Jamal's opponent reach at him, prompting Jamal to attack with a football tackle. He hit him at his waist and lifted his legs onto the mat, going down with him and controlling him on the mat. "2 takedown," said the referee. His opponent turned from his back to his belly and immediately stood up. Jamal remembered this – "follow and lift." When his opponent stood, Jamal followed him to his feet, and then lifted him up with his waist and took him right back down to the mat. The Warren kid stood again. Ditto. Follow and lift. *I got the hang of this, as long as the kid stands up.* When the kid landed on his belly, the bench started yelling, "Half! Half!" Clueless.

Jamal had no idea what they were talking about. Instead he just pushed and pulled his opponent, trying to get him onto his back again. It was sheer muscling and not wrestling that Jamal was doing. *This kid is not so strong after all.*

The first period ended. It was Jamal's choice. He looked to Coach Russo. Pointing down, Coach Russo told him, "Down, tell him down."

The referee told Jamal to take the down position. He then told the Warren kid to get on top. The whistle blew, and Jamal was up in a flash and away from his opponent. "1 point escape," said the referee. Jamal didn't know the match score; he dared not take his eyes off his opponent. He believed he was winning. He was winning. It was 7-1. Two minutes into his wrestling career and he already had two takedowns, one nearfall and one escape. Confidence was brewing. As he circled his opponent, though not as frenetically as before, he thought to himself: *Bear hug. Worked once. Maybe it will again.* He rushed his opponent, grabbing him under his arms again and squeezing him into him and taking him right to his back again. This time he had a bit more control. The referee jumped to the mat, awarded Jamal's takedown points and eyed the Warren kid's back. Jamal couldn't hold him down. The two rolled out of bounds, and the referee stopped the action and brought them back to the center. "Warren, you're down," said the ref. Jamal heard Coach Russo. He looked toward him.

"Let him up and take him down again."

"What?" Why would Jamal just let him up?

"Just do it," ordered Coach Russo.

Jamal took his place atop his opponent. The referee blew the whistle, and Jamal did as he was told. He let his opponent go. As soon as he was on his feet, Jamal attacked his legs again. "2 points takedown," said the ref.

"Let him up again," said Coach Russo.

He did. And took him down again. "Do it again." And he did. All this down and up was starting to get to Jamal. His breathing was deep, his muscles as taut as a guitar string. His mouth was very dry. There was another period to go. *When did two minutes get so long?*

Jamal was not as energetic the last period, but he did enough to win. When the final whistle ended the match, Jamal felt like collapsing. The referee brought the two wrestlers to the center of the circle and raised Jamal's hand in the air. Jamal ran to the opposing coach and shook his hand, just as he had seen his teammates do at the end of their matches.

Coach Russo's extended hand awaited him when he returned to the Kennedy bench. "Congratulations, Jamal. You're 1-0 for your career. And on two days of practice. Not one technical violation the whole match. You went the entire six minutes. We might have found something you're pretty good at." He patted Jamal on the head and told him to go get a sip from the water fountain. "How do you feel?" he asked before letting him go.

"Tired. That last period seemed like an hour," answered Jamal.

"Yeah, but you made it. We get you in shape and teach you a little, you'll be alright."

"Yes sir. Hope so."

Jamal's teammates all congratulated him on his win. He ran to the water fountain and returned to his seat on the bench. He looked in the stands. There were many classmates he recognized. He didn't' know their names, but he knew their faces. In the middle rows, he saw his grandfather. He'd made it to the match. Jamal hadn't seen him earlier. The tunnel-vision created by his nerves wouldn't let him.

Jamal watched the few remaining matches and cheered the teammates, whose names he didn't know, on in their matches. Then the match was done. Both teams lined up facing each other in single file lines and walked across the mat, shaking the hand of each wrestler who passed by them. This was followed by several minutes of talking to parents, classmates and even the Warren wrestlers.

Coach Russo then gathered the team on the mat. "A good night guys. Great job varsity. And let's hear it for Jamal. Two days of work and he gets a win." The team clapped their approval. Jamal felt a bit embarrassed by the attention, though deep inside he enjoyed it greatly.

Coach Russo continued: "Freshmen and JV. Break down the room and put everything up. Tomorrow is a practice day. Be here on time."

The team gave a last breakdown before going about cleaning up the room.

Jamal got dressed, turned in his uniform and shoes. Coach Russo told him to keep the shoes. On his way out of the locker room, Coach Russo once again told, "Great job out there. You did very well. Make sure you're here tomorrow. You'll be sore and will need the stretching. I'm gonna' set aside some time to work with you one on one after practice. Big tournament on Saturday. See you tomorrow."

"Yes sir." Jamal exited the locker room and saw his grandfather waiting on the bleachers.

"Boy," he said, "I don't know nothing about wrestling, but you looked like you were pretty tough. You put a good whuppin' on that kid. That kid was bigger than you and all, but you threw him around like a rag doll."

"I didn't make weight, so I had to go against that big guy."

"Yeah, well it didn't matter too much. You put it on him good. What you mean you didn't make weight? How much you got to weigh?"

"152 pounds. I came in at 154. I had to go up a weight class."

"We'll fix that. Get you on a good diet, starting tonight."

"Yes sir, Pop."

As the two exited the gym, Lonny Hayes patted Jamal on his head. "I'm proud of you boy. You done good out there."

— SEVEN —

The next morning's announcements were led off with the results of the wrestling team's victory over Warren High School. Coach Russo made the announcement himself. Midway through the announcement, Jamal perked up: "And in his first match ever, with only two days of practice, freshman Jamal Hayes defeated his opponent 18-6. Good job Jamal!" Jamal's name on the school intercom – and it wasn't to report to the office for some infraction or another.

His classmates high-fived him, while his homeroom teacher, Ms. Phillips, told him, "Good job." While a bit embarrassed by the attention, Jamal again had to admit he liked it.

Throughout the day, Jamal received congratulations in the freshmen hallway. His older teammates offered the same at lunch. Less than a week at his new school, and things couldn't be any better. Unusual territory for Jamal.

Kennedy High School, like literally every high school in the country, had its cliques, often with an urban edge. Derrick clued him in a bit at lunch: "We got the athletes. There's the weed crowd. There's the crowd that sells the dope to the weed crowd. You got the geeks, the thugs – more wannabe than anything else – and the bad folks, the ones to stay away from." He meant gangs. "They run the hallways everyday. I don't mean 'run,' as in control, I mean run as in physically running the hallways. They come to school each morning and spend the entire day looking around corners for the principals. They never go to class. Coach says to ignore 'em and stay away from'em. Says these type people only drag you down to their level. I'm cool with 'em. But I don't hang out with 'em. Too busy. You don't need to either. Ninth grade is where most of 'em are. They stir up all the trouble. Just stay away from 'em."

Jamal listened to Derrick. In Chicago, he'd probably have been one of those Derrick was speaking of. He'd try to avoid that group if he could.

The entire school was different than his school in Chicago. Yes, there were similarities. The hallways in between classes were often chaotic with profanity filling the air, but there were stark contrasts too. Many of the students actually worked in class; going to the principal's office was actually a *bad* thing here, something to be feared. During the classes, the hallways were largely empty.

Such was not the case back home in Chicago. The school police ran his old school. The school system had its own police force with arresting authority. They ran the hallways in their orange jackets. A book in his old Chicago school was merely a projectile to be hurled at someone. Class periods were 50 minute "check sessions," with students trying to out-check each other in each new period. The hallways were always filled with students, even with the police in the halls. It mattered none to some if they were thrown out of school with a suspension or even an expulsion. Each meant time away from the school, something everyone wanted. If you got a referral slip to the office, it became nothing more than a virtual hall pass to let you wander all you wanted, or allowed you to slip out one of the school's exits.

Yes, Kennedy High School was much different than his old Chicago school.

At 2:15, the bell ended the day's lessons, and the doors opened, emptying the students into the streets surrounding Kennedy. The wrestling team headed to practice room for another day's work. The city of Memphis came to mean work for Jamal. Whether it was at his grandfather's house or at school, he worked – at least, he had since he started wrestling three days ago. In the classroom and out on the mat, he was working hard. While he wasn't crazy about the list of chores his grandfather had for him daily or the workload of his classes, he did enjoy the "work" of wrestling practice. Certainly, it was physically difficult, but, as last night had proven, it carried with it some rewards: winning and having your hand raised in the air. He couldn't explain it. He didn't get any money for wrestling, but that feeling of winning was great. He looked forward to Saturday's tournament for the opportunity to win again.

Coach Russo blew the whistle for the start of the day. It was 3:00 straight up. The man was consistent. He started the same time each day, not one minute later.

Coach brought the group to order. "First, great job last night. Varsity, we drilled 'em, just like it was designed. We're 3-0, a good start, but it's just the beginning of a long year. As we get more into the season, the busier and tougher things will get. It's the first week of December. Lot of time between now and February, so let's take things one match a time, one week at a time.

"Secondly, you new guys did a great job too. And you got a big event on Saturday. Those guys you beat last night, they'll be looking to get you back. If you lost last night, Saturday is a chance to get revenge. That's what's great about wrestling. There's always another chance to get back at someone who beat you.

He paused for effect, to let his words settle on the guys' minds. "We're gonna' do something a bit different today. You know me. I like to keep you guys on your toes. Change things up a bit. We're gonna' spend the first half of practice in the weight room, and then we'll hit the mat for a little sweat."

Coach told the team to get in groups of four according to weight class. He then marched the groups into the weight room, which was housed in an old locker room that was located in a basement under the gym. All the lockers had been removed, leaving just the vacant floor, which was now covered in black rubber matting. It was hot and cramped, and it also had every sort of weight station you could imagine: two bench presses, one incline bench, two squat racks, one cleans rack, sit-up benches, dips bars, and a pull-up station. One side of the small room had mirrors, while the other was lined up with a rack of dumbbells.

The groups were each at a station. Coach instructed each quartet to do two sets of twelve at each station with everybody doing the same weight. He would time each station and blow the whistle to signal the time to move to another station.

Jamal had never done squats or cleans. He had a hard time getting the form of each exercise. He kept using his back to lift instead of the legs. He watched each of the guys in his group and tired to do as they did. It didn't work. Two sets of each just wasn't enough time to learn all this new stuff. He barely did ten of the squats and just three of the cleans. Lifting weights was not as easy as he thought it would be.

The older wrestlers ripped through their sets as if they'd been doing them since birth. Derrick, the team's captain and best wrestler, cleaned two sets of 225 pounds with ease. He was strong. Even more amazing for Jamal was watching 130 pound Andre bench press 200 pounds like it was 20 pounds. For that matter, all the lighter weight guys on the varsity team worked out with heavy weight. And Jamal couldn't even squat 180 pounds. He could only bench 135 pounds. Coach Russo's words came back to him: "Keep on working, and you'll get it."

Jamal's group rotated to the other stations of the workout. He did well on some of them and not so well on others. The dips were tough, as were the pull-ups. The upright rows were easier to do, but the dumbbell lunges were killers. His thighs burned, and he was only doing 20 pounds in each hand.

After and hour and a half, Coach Russo had the team back in the wrestling room and on the mat. Jamal thought, *There's no way we're gonna' do a full practice now. My arms and legs are gone.*

It wasn't a full practice. A little loosening up was followed in brief succession by four rounds of jump rope, mat drills and, of course, push-ups and sit-ups. A two-minute water break was followed by live work on the mat: four man rotations, takedowns, top work and bottom work.

Coach Russo blew his whistle. "That's an hour and fifteen minute workout," he told the group, "just like I like it. Upbeat, fast paced, lots of moving." He paused a second and then told the varsity to get on one half of the mat and the new guys on the other half. "We had some weight issues last night. Couple of folks got greedy with the donuts and didn't make weight." He looked at the varsity half of the mat and pointed at a wrestler. "Ronald, you're on that half of the mat with the varsity. Jamal, you're on the half with the new guys." Jamal had no idea what was going on. "Firedrill!" Coach Russo yelled.

Jamal still had no idea what "firedrill" meant. He'd learn in seconds, as Coach Russo simply explained it: "Jamal, you take on every one of the new guys, and Ronald, you take on all varsity. And keep it goin' 'til I say stop. Takedowns."

Coach Russo blew the whistle. The JV guys lined up one after the other on the edge of the mat. The first wrestler, a 112 pounder, squared up with Jamal. Jamal circled, then feinted his right hand, and shot in for a double leg takedown. The moment he was on his feet, his next opponent in the line was in his face. Jamal got that takedown also, which was followed by another opponent. Jamal continued with this drill until he had gone through everyone, including the big 250 pound heavyweight. That meant ten guys, of which he won the first two takedowns, and then he began to slow. By the time he reached the middle weight guys – 145, 152, and 160 – he was gassed. When the big 250 pound ninth grade heavyweight came on the mat, the takedown was less than competitive. Jamal practically fell to the mat. His wind was gone. Jamal could barely get up, when the 112 pounder was back in his face. Jamal slowly stood, and the 112 pound sophomore attacked him, taking him down with a single leg takedown. "As soon as he stands up, get on him," Coach Russo instructed the other JV wrestlers. And they did. When the heavyweight wrestler appeared in front of Jamal for the second go-round, he literally had to pick Jamal up from the mat only to take him down again. Russo kept a stop watch in his hand as he observed the drill. "Let's go Jamal," he said, "you're not getting off that mat until you get three takedowns in a row." Jamal struggled to his feet. He gasped for breath, but it was eluding him. The 119 pounder took him down with ease. He again struggled to his feet, only to be met by the JV 125 pound wrestler. Jamal couldn't even get into a stance before he found himself on the mat again, taken down by a smaller wrestler. After what seemed like an hour – actually it was only five minutes – Coach Russo blew his whistle twice, signaling the end of Jamal's torture. He told everyone to circle up for the end of the day. Before he got to his final comments of the day, he looked at Jamal and said, "Make your weight. I've got some diet tips and a list of food in the office. I'll give you one at the end of the day. Don't show up fat for matches." After the five-minute beat-down he'd just experienced, Jamal was getting that sheet of paper and going on a diet.

"New guys, we have a tournament on Saturday. I have the entry forms. Take one and pass them around." He handed the forms to one of the wrestlers sitting in the front. "There's an entry fee. It's seven dollars. Most important of all is to get the form signed by your parents and show up on Saturday, entry fee with you or not. Be here at the school at 6:30 Saturday morning. Bus will leave at 6:45. Don't be late. We'll be there all day. It's at St. Paul, a private school out east. Tell your folks in case they want to come.

"Hour and fifteen minute practice and weight check tomorrow. It's Friday, so don't go getting a case of 'Friday-it is' and not show up. I'd hate to have to get rid of any of you. Be here on time tomorrow, and let's get it done. Cool it down, and let's go home."

The team did its end of the day cool down and headed to the locker room for the weight check. Jamal was covered in sweat. When it was his turn on the scale, he stepped on. "153.1," said Coach Russo. "You're a pound and a tenth over. Practice tomorrow, and you should be at or under 152 pounds. Remember, if you don't make weight on Saturday, you'll have to bump up and go 160 pounds, not to mention another firedrill on Monday. It ain't so good going against those big boys. We can't tell where you're at. Plus, I know you don't want to have to be firedrilled again. Be at 152 on Saturday. Here, take this with you. It is a list of good stuff to eat and not so good stuff to eat."

Jamal took the sheet of paper and looked it over. Coach Russo continued: "There's plenty of stuff you can eat. I bet you have some of that stuff at home now, or you could get hold of some it tonight. Don't worry too much. You'll learn about diet and the way you need to eat. You've only been out less than a week. You'll get it. Diet, training, studying, and rest – it all goes together in wrestling. Wrestling is not a sport as much as it is a lifestyle, one that you live from November until February. You make your weight on Saturday, and I bet you'll do great. Believe me, you got it. I've seen 'it,' and you got 'it.'" Now go home and get some rest, and I'll see you tomorrow."

"Yes sir," said Jamal. He walked out to his grandfather, who was waiting for him in the parking lot.

— EIGHT —

Unlike a team meet with just two or maybe three teams, a wrestling tournament is huge affair with up to sixteen teams and can last all day or even the better part of two days. Typically held on Saturdays, tournaments begin early in the morning with weigh-ins and finish sometime that night with the consolation and championship finals and the awards ceremony with the top four in each weight class getting an Olympic-like medal for their performances that day. Fourteen weight classes means there are only 56 medals up for grabs, and everyone – sometimes 150 plus wrestlers – is trying to get one of the medals.

The gym floor at St. Paul was covered with three mats, and wrestlers from the sixteen schools at the tournament were scattered across the four mats, warming up in any number of ways. Some entire teams jogged single file around the mats, while other teams took their own section of a mat as their practice area. Teams had staked out various sections of the bleachers as "their" seats for the day. Jamal, like the rest of his Kennedy teammates, was amazed with the St. Paul gymnasium. The place looked more like a modern new college gymnasium instead of a high school gym. It had fixed bleachers rather than the retracting ones Kennedy High had. Outside the gym's doors was a huge entry hallway, complete with huge trophy cases that were filled with trophies for every sport imaginable, even some sports Jamal didn't know were in high school: lacrosse, swimming, rugby and equestrian. *Equestrian. What is that? And why are there horses on those trophies?* he thought.

There were even tables in the concession stand area. The concession stand itself resembled more of a restaurant than a concession stand. The entire school screamed "money" in a big way.

The Kennedy kids, all dressed in their blue warm-ups – Jamal had been given a used warm-up from last season – were on the mats with the other associated colors of the participating schools. Coach Russo had told them to stay warm because the event would be starting soon. He had earlier taken his freshmen out to the great atrium to show each wrestler his bracket for the day's competition. Jamal didn't know what to make of his. It looked kind of like the "March Madness" brackets he had seen his teachers complete during the NCAA basketball tournament each March. Coach Russo clued Jamal and the rest of team in on the brackets: "It's a double elimination tournament, meaning you have to lose twice before you are eliminated. Each of you will get at least two matches today. If we perform like I know we can, each of you will probably get more than two. I want each of you to win every match so I can see you on that medal stand tonight. Gold medals for everyone!" Kennedy brought twelve freshmen to the tournament. While not a full lineup of fourteen wrestlers, it was enough of a group to score a lot of team points and finish in the top three or four of the competing schools.

Jamal made his weight today, but not without some worry. When he'd weighed himself at the school before leaving Kennedy, he'd weighed 153.2 pounds, a little bit over. Two other Kennedy wrestlers were in the same boat. "Not to worry," said Coach Russo, "get your warm-ups on before we get on the bus. Sit with me at the front of the bus." All three overweight wrestlers did as they were told. About a mile and a half from St. Paul,

Coach Russo told the bus driver to pull over to the side of the street. "Get out," he told the overweight threesome. "Start running that way, and you'll run right into the school. Get on it; I want you there in ten minutes. We all have to weigh in together, so don't be late." The door closed, and the bus pulled away. Jamal and his two teammates started jogging in the direction Coach Russo said. In moments, they picked up their pace. One of the wrestlers had a timer on his watch. He kept time, checking it every minute or so. Each wrestler had his backpack or gym bag with them, and the extra load was strapped to each in some fashion. The three reached the school in 9:43 seconds, just in time to catch up with the team, which was at the school's door about to enter. "Glad you could make it," said Coach Russo. Each of the Kennedy wrestlers stepped on the scale, and each made weight. Jamal checked in at 151.9 pounds, just one-tenth under 152 pounds. Running to the tournament or match site was coach's way of handling any overweight wrestlers. He'd been doing this for years.

Thirteen schools from all over the Memphis area, both public and private, were at the tournament, as were two schools from Arkansas and one from Nashville. Each mat had a Roman numeral on it to let the wrestlers know which mat they'd be wrestling on.

Coach Russo gathered the team on one corner of one of the mats and told them what to expect: "The announcer will call out you and your opponent's names. They'll tell you to come to the head table. It's over there" – he pointed to a long table against one wall of the gym – "You'll go there, and they'll give you a bout sheet and tell what mat you need to go to. Once at the mat, you'll either be 'in the hole,' meaning two matches are ahead of you or you'll be 'on deck,' which means your match is next. The minute that you get to your mat, start stretching and loosening up. If I am not there immediately, don't worry, I will be. Got twelve of you and one of me." Jayson and the other guys who helped Coach Russo couldn't make it today. "I might have two or three going at the same time. I will get a spot where you can see me. Feeling the team's nervous edge, he added, "Remember, this is a freshman tournament. These guys are just like you. Many of them are first year guys too. Some may have experience, but they don't have much more than you. And don't sweat the fancy uniforms and warm-ups, this fantastic gym or the crowd – none of it matters. None of it. The only thing that matters is that you bring it when that referee blows that whistle. Get after it, and we'll do fine." Jamal and the team felt a bit more relaxed after coach spoke.

"One more thing guys. Tournaments like this will start with the lower weight classes and move up in order. Some of you will be waiting for a while before your first match. It'll speed up once the first round is done. Pay attention to the announcers. Listen for your name and weight class. You lighter guys, get ready and warm-up now."

Moments later, an announcer's voice filled the air: "All wrestlers, clear the mats!"

The Kennedy team took its place in the bleachers. The team's smallest wrestler, Michael Barnes, was warming up when his name was called. He and Coach Russo walked to the head table and got the bout sheet and reported to mat number two. Theodore Kirby, Kennedy's 112 pounder, had his name called minutes later, and he reported to the head table. He was sent to mat number three.

Michael Barnes was small, but he was fast and strong, especially when you consider he only weighed 100 pounds. He didn't know much wrestling, but his strength made up for his lack of knowledge. Jamal had wrestled with him at practice the day before, and he was amazed at how strong Michael was. It took all of Jamal's strength to take Michael down and control him. Michael's first round opponent was no match for Michael. The starting whistle was followed instantly by Michael locking up with his opponent in a collar-elbow tie, with Michael moving his opponent around the mat a few seconds before perfectly executing an ankle pick, which had Michael's opponent on his back and quickly pinned. Michael got up, took off his red ankle band, and ran to the head table to sign his bout sheet before taking it back to the head table. Michael pinned his opponent in :21 seconds.

Just as Michael had his hand raised, Coach Russo rushed to mat three to be in Theo's corner. Theo's match was on deck and would be on the mat in moments. Theo was built much like Michael, compact and muscular. Theo liked the bear-hug. Coach Russo had told him over and over to get another move to go with his favorite, but Theo was headstrong. It wouldn't matter this match, as the moment the whistle was blown, Theo rushed his opponent, grabbed him in a bear-hug and tripped him to his back. The referee slapped the mat moments later. Another pin for the Kennedy wrestling team. "Two wins, no losses," Coach Russo said as he left the mat, patting Theo on the back.

Jamal and his teammates tried to get as close to each mat every time a Kennedy wrestler was competing. They all shouted encouragement, yelling certain moves out to their teammate – moves most had just learned themselves. It mattered not that many had not mastered the move; they nonetheless shouted like experts.

Jamal's coaching was interrupted by the tournament announcer: "Jamal Hayes, Kennedy High School to the head table.' With two teammates in tow, Jamal made his way to the head table, where his opponent, adorned in a maroon sweatshirt, awaited him. The two were given the bout sheet and headed to mat number four.

While his teammates warmed him up, Jamal's nerves kicked back into high gear, the same nerves that he thought had disappeared with his first win two nights previous. One of his teammates pulled his arms behind him to loosen his shoulders, while another gave him instructions on what to do when the match started. Still another gave him a jump rope and told him to get a light sweat going. "Get a little sweat worked up," Coach

Russo had told the team earlier. Coach Russo soon joined Jamal. "You keep moving. I'll get to you when it's time." Two matches were ahead of Jamal, so he had plenty of time to get warm.

Nerves, he thought. Weren't a problem until I heard my name – I liked hearing my name. As soon as the announcer called Jamal's name out over the gym's PA system, a wave of angst swept over him. The "jitters" returned to every part of his body. His mind was crowded and his vision seemingly stuck in a tunnel. He'd planned his whole strategy for this match, had it all worked out. And now he was blank. The plan pushed aside by his questions. *What if this guy is real good? What if the guy is stronger than me? What if I get hurt?* The questions seemingly caused him to lose his peripheral vision. While focus is a good thing, it can be a detriment if it leads to tunnel vision. Focus allows an athlete to compete at his best, while tunnel vision, created by being nervous, hampers even the best athlete's performance.

Jamal was now "on deck," meaning his match was next. As he took off his sweatshirt and gym shorts and affixed his headgear, Coach Russo came to his side: "How do you feel?"

"Good," answered Jamal, still somewhat moving in place and shaking his legs out one at a time.

"This is just like the other night. We just got a bigger crowd and it's for real. Keep things simple. Do the things you know and don't get creative or adventuresome. When you take him down, look to grab his waist real tight and stay behind him. Try to get him flat, just like we have told you at practice. I saw you doing things perfectly yesterday. Get him flat and look for the half-nelson. If he takes you down, immediately get to your feet and tear free."

Jamal nodded his head.

"Remember how you did the other night? Take him down and let him up? Same here. If you take him down to the mat, and nothing's there, let him up and take him down again. Keep it simple. Look to me on the breaks, and we'll get you through it. You're gonna' do fine."

That match on the mat ended with a pin. Coach Russo told Jamal to check in with the scorer's table. "They'll tell what color ankle band to put on. They're out on the mat." Jamal was told he was red. He went to the center of the mat and put the red ankle band on. Coach Russo signaled for him to come to the corner for a second. "Listen, on that first whistle, go get him. Jump on him like he stole something. Think right now what you want to do and let it go when the referee blows his whistle." Jamal nodded his head and went to the center of the mat.

The referee brought the two combatants to the center, told them to shake hands, checked with the scorer's table and blew the whistle.

Jamal's opponent acted first, shooting for Jamal's legs and the takedown. Jamal answered with a quick sprawl, his legs extended back and his hips on his opponent's shoulders. Just as quickly, he moved around and behind his opponent for the takedown. *How'd I do that?* "Two takedown, red,: said the referee. Jamal went to work. He held his opponent's waist and reached with his left hand under his opponent for his far arm. He had it by the tricep. He then released his opponent's belly and drew his near hand to his opponent's near ankle. Once he secured his opponent's ankle, he pulled the tricep and the ankle, causing his opponent to roll onto his back, where he struggled to get back to his "base," his hands and knees. Jamal tried to secure him on his back, but was unable to keep from turning back onto his belly. He went right back to the same move, and he had his opponent back on his back. The referee signaled the back points and Jamal squeezed. He was able to "T-up" his body, meaning keep his body at such an angle that the two forms created a "T" shape. His opponent could not hook his legs if done properly, plus the angle created by the "T" allowed for more pressure to be applied from the top position.

Jamal's opponent was able to scoot himself out of bounds, causing the referee to blow his whistle and bring the two back to the center. "Green, you're down," said the ref, pointing to the center circle for the wrestler to take his down position on the small lines in the center circle. "Ready," asked the referee. Jamal's opponent nodded okay. "Top," said the referee, pointing to Jamal. Jamal took his place in the referee's position on top. The whistle blew. Jamal's opponent stood up and tore free, and the referee signaled one point for the escape. The two wrestlers circled each other. No quick shots this time from the kid. Jamal circled and feinted at his opponent with his left hand, causing him to reach a little with his hands. Jamal was feeling more confident now. He faked again with his left hand. When his opponent reached with his arms, Jamal shot under his reach and attacked his hips with a perfectly executed double-leg takedown. Jamal had his opponent flat on his back, and the referee counted. In seconds, the referee blew his whistle and slapped the mat. Match over. Another Kennedy win. Jamal was now undefeated. Of course, 2-0 was not necessarily a daunting streak of wins, but it was undefeated nonetheless.

As he walked off the mat, Jamal noticed that feeling again, the same one Jamal had felt on Wednesday night. Victory. It felt even better this time.

Coach Russo shook his hand and offered up, "Good job. Now let's get the next one."

The tournament continued, making its way to the heavier weight classes and the second round. At the end of the first round of the tournament, the Kennedy wrestlers were 11-1. Only their 171-pound wrestler lost his first round match, but he was still alive with just one loss. *We're pretty good, Jamal thought.*

The tournament dragged on. Wrestling tournaments did that. There's excitement at the first part and the medal rounds, but the middle portion is like the long 162 game season the major leagues, on and on with no seeming end in sight, much like a boring class lecture.

Jamal won his second and third round matches, felling a little more comfortable and confident with each win. Every additional minute he spent on the mat is information added to his know-how. Every move mastered in a match was now in his "tool-box." Just like Coach Russo told them it would be: "When you do a move in a match, you own it."

Jamal's Kennedy teammates did very well also. It was into the semi-finals now, and Kennedy had eight wrestlers in the semis. If each won his semi-final match, the team would have eight going for gold medals. The other four wrestlers were still alive in the consolation bracket. Kennedy could place everyone, meaning everyone could walk out of the gym with a medal, and the team would definitely finish in the top three of the tourney field. Coach Russo noticed it also: "If we keep up like this, we could walk out of here with a lot of hardware—medals and even a team trophy. It could be a real good day for us."

When it came time for Jamal's semi-final match, the Kennedy wrestlers were 5-0 in semi-final matches. Jamal's opponent was a redheaded kid from Davidson High School in Nashville. Wearing a solid black singlet, the kid was built like a tank: short and powerful. He was shorter than Jamal, but he was much thicker in the chest and legs. The kid looked like he'd been on steroids since third grade. The two eyed each other warily, as each bounced around the warm-up area. Coach Russo was by Jamal's side. He watched the other 152-pound semi-final, scouting each of the potential opponents. "Jamal," he said, "you get the winner." Did Coach Russo forget that Jamal had to beat the Nashville kid first?

The match in front of Jamal's entered its third period. Coach Russo grabbed Jamal and pulled him aside. "Listen, don't be fooled by the looks of someone. This kid you got to wrestle. He looks all strong and stuff, but don't buy it. I watched him earlier. He's not that good, just tries to muscle folks around. Half the folks he wrestles are scared before they get out there. You don't do that. Go after him like you've done everyone else. That kid will quit. He's like a bully. When he sees that you ain't backing down, he'll throw in the towel. Believe me. I've seen it happen a hundred times with these muscle boys. This kid ain't been past the first period today. Drag him into the 'deep water,' and watch him drown. Go after him hard, rough him up. We get him to the second period, and he is done. Simple."

Coach Russo was right. The kid from Nashville, while muscled up, was not a good wrestler. Turns out he was a first year wrestler also. He was not as strong as he looked either. Jamal, in fact, had an easy time with him and actually muscled him around the mat. He had a relatively easy time with the Nashville kid, beating him 14-3. Once the match got into the second period, the kid was running out of gas. He was strong, but it was like the muscles were a costume and not real. One minute into the match, Jamal knew he had him and trounced him the rest of the way, taking him down, trying new moves out and letting him up. He put the kid on his back several times and held him there, only to let him roll out of bounds or let him up, where Jamal would repeat the process. He could've pinned him, but he has yet to master the art of holding an opponent down on his back for the pin. More work to be done. At least, he was beginning to look like he knew what he was doing. In less than a week of wrestling, he was 4-0 – 5-0, if you count the Wednesday exhibition – and assured of finishing, at least, second place in his first real tournament. Less than a month earlier, he was doing his best impersonation of a budding dropout and hoodlum on the South Side of Chicago, completely unaware of the athlete inside of him that was dying to get out.

The Kennedy team had seven wrestlers in the championship finals, five in the consolation semi-finals and currently sitting in third place in the team standings. A good performance in the medal round could see the team finish in second place. First would be great, but with weight classes missing, it would be difficult to get first place. Before the medal round began, Coach Russo gathered the team together on section of one of the mats: "Take a knee guys and listen. I think we got third placed sewed up, but if we do well in this round, we might be able to get the runner-up trophy. We have done a great job so far, but our work is not done yet. We can't win the tournament, but, hey, all these people" – he paused and waved his hands toward the crowd in the stands – "know that with a full lineup, we'd take that championship trophy. Not bad for a small school from Frayser." Coach Russo's words from earlier in the day came back to the team: "Forget the fancy uniforms, the fancy gym. It only matters what you do on the mat."

The Kennedy team held on – barely – to third place. Of the seven Kennedy wrestlers in the finals, just three captured the gold medal. Jamal wasn't one of them. The nerves got him, as did a very good opponent from North High School, a public school just outside of Memphis: Colin Young. Jamal couldn't do anything against Young. Every move he tried, the North wrestler answered it with a counter. Outclassed is the word. Jamal had heard it on ESPN once to describe a team that was thoroughly beaten in a basketball game. The word was appropriate, as Colin Young gave Jamal a lesson in wrestling. Jamal was pinned in the second period, and he was lucky to last until the second period. Young played with him, it seemed, the first period, much like Jamal had done with his Nashville opponent in the semi-finals. It was the first time he had lost in a real sport, and he didn't like it. As good as he felt in victory, he felt even worse in defeat; it was all so personal. He felt the entire crowd's eyes were on him, and he felt so self-conscious. They were watching a *loser.* Even the rewarding of his second place medal on the medal stand did little to erase the self-inflicted shame Jamal felt. Coach Russo's words of congratulation fell short of their goal; Jamal felt awful. Jamal wasn't a bad sport, but he, at least on the inside, wasn't a gracious loser either. He hated losing and wished he could have been able to wrestle Colin Young again as they stood on the medal stand. *Like Coach Russo said, "There'll be another day."* That day couldn't come soon enough for Jamal.

Coach Russo was so optimistic about the entire group. Before the bus left the St. Paul parking lot, he told the team how good a job they had done that day. Some of his comments were aimed at, it seemed, Jamal, in particular: "If you lost today, and you didn't like it, good. Never get used to losing or accept it. Losing is a habit, one you don't want to adopt. Before long, you accept it, and it's over then, not just in wrestling, but in life. Always get back up and keep going. Always. You guys will get another shot at these guys maybe at the city tournament. Remember the loss, and avenge it then. We'll do the work to get it back starting on Monday. Until then, celebrate this. It is a great day to be a Kennedy wrestler. Ten medals – two wrestlers lost in the consolation semi-finals – going back to Frayser, with more to come in the future. Three gold medals, four silver, three third place finishes and one fourth ain't too bad for a group of first year wrestlers. You guys did well. I'm proud of each of you. Let's go home."

The bus pulled out of St. Paul and started the long trek down I-240 to Frayser. It was a good forty-five minute drive from the school, which was located on the extreme east side of Memphis. Ten minutes into the drive, snores could be heard coming from the back of the bus. It was approaching 10:00 PM, and the team had been up since before 6 AM that morning. It was a long and taxing day.

The bus suddenly stopped, waking up the slumbering grapplers. "Wake up," said Coach Russo. The wrestlers stirred, one asking, "Are we already home?" The bus was in front of pizza parlor in Germantown, a city just outside of Memphis. "Let's go celebrate a bit," Coach Russo said, getting off the bus. The team followed him. As they entered the restaurant, Jamal sidled up to Coach Russo. "Coach, I don't have any money with me, so I'll just get some water and sit."

"Don't worry about it. I got this. I promised you guys if all of you won your weight class, I'd buy some pizza. We didn't do that, but we did do a good job. Enjoy it. Just don't eat too much of it. One piece for you 'donut boys' that had to run this morning."

The team did just that, but not too much. Coach Russo did monitor their eating, allowing just two pieces per wrestler, except for the "donut boys." Call Jamal "Mr. Krispy Kreme." The team sat at their table and talked of the day's events, both congratulating and joshing with teammates. The mockery was a good-natured and all in fun. Coach Russo mostly sat in silence and watched his team enjoy themselves.

The bus got back to Kennedy at 11:30. Jamal's grandfather, as well as the other parents of the team members, was waiting in the parking lot. Coach Russo spoke with each parent before they left. He told them of the good job the team had done and about practice on Monday. He shook hands with Lonny and said, "I think we got a good one here, Mr. Hayes. He was outstanding today, taking second place at a tough tournament." Jamal had his second place medal hanging around his neck with a blue ribbon.

Lonny Hayes got into his truck and looked at Jamal. "Second place, huh?"

"Yes sir. Next time, I'll get first."

"They sho' keep you out a long time today."

"We were at the school all day. I guess that how these things go. Coach Russo took us out to get pizza after we were done. We got third as a team, so he let us celebrate a little."

"Second place. Sounds like done found yourself a talent."

"Yes sir. I guess I have."

The two drove home in silence. No surprise. Lonny Hayes didn't talk much anyway, and Jamal's full day – all 14 hours of it – had caught up with him, causing him to nod off before they got home. At 11:45 PM – Jamal saw it on his clock – sleep overtook him, his last thought being his silver medal and how it would be gold the next time he was in a tournament.

— Nine —

The fight started suddenly, but it had been brewing since homeroom. Jamal did just as Coach Russo told him – walk away from confrontation or trouble…unless someone puts his hands on you. Jamal walked away for most of the day, ignoring the insults and threats. When the first hand was put on him though, he acted quickly, almost instinctively, with a double-leg takedown to the ground, followed by an array of punches to the boy's head, all while holding his foe down with his other hand. It was over in a matter of seconds. "Henry," his attacker, never had a chance. The students in the hallway, as they always did when a confrontation turned physical, ran to the fight, circling around the combatants, making a ring of sorts. It was over as quickly as it had begun, with two male teachers intervening, separating the two and carting them down to the office.

Mr. Griffith awaited the two in his office. Jamal felt a sense of dread come over him: What was going to happen now? At his Chicago school, any fisticuffs were followed by a trip to the juvenile detention facility for both involved in such. Jamal didn't want to go to jail. He was just defending himself. A trip downtown would most certainly end his wrestling, something he had come to like a lot. There was no way his grandfather would let him wrestle if he was sent to jail. What would Coach Russo say?

Jamal didn't imagine he would be pleased with this, even though Jamal did exactly what his coach had told him.

While Jamal and Henry waited in two chairs just outside Mr. Griffith's office, Jamal saw Officer Peterson, the school's police officer, enter the office to speak with Mr. Griffith. This was not good, thought Jamal. He was certain that handcuffs and a perp walk through the halls on his way to the squad car were on tap. Dang, he thought, why didn't I just walk away?

In minutes that seemed like hours, Mr. Griffith called both the boys into his office. He wanted to get their side. One at a time, each boy was asked what happened and told his tale. Jamal's version was the truth, while Henry's version was a story was some sort of foreign adventure; the two's stories were opposite the other's. "I am going to assume," Mr. Griffith started, "that the truth lies somewhere in the middle of these two very different stories." He paused a moment. "So Jamal you say that you did nothing whatsoever until Henry bumped into you and pushed you during the break before lunch, correct?"

"Yes sir," he answered.

"And Henry, you say that Jamal just attacked you without provocation?"

"What is provocation?" asked Henry.

"Comes from the word 'provoke," means Jamal started things."

"Yeah, that's it. He started it all. I didn't do 'nuthin'."

"That's a lie. That's not true. I got witnesses," Jamal quickly answered.

"I see. Okay, you boys go into the office and call your folks. Sit and wait for them in the office."

The two boys did as told. Lonny was none too enthused to receive the call. He told Jamal he would be there shortly, and he was, a grim look on his face. It was the same look he had when Jamal got off the plane a few weeks back. He said nothing, until the two were ensconced in two chairs in Mr. Griffith's office.

"Mr. Hayes, good to see you again," said Mr. Griffith, extending his hand. Jamal's grandfather said nothing. When he had taken his seat, Mr. Griffith looked at Jamal: "Jamal, why don't you tell me your side of things."

"I was just walking down the hall. The kid bumped into me, and I kept on walking. He then put his hands on me and pushed me in the back. I almost fell. When I got up, he was coming at me, so I just reacted. Several of his friends tried to get involved, but some people held them back."

"That would be a couple of the wrestlers," said the principal. "Go on."

"I just reacted and did what it took to protect myself. I wasn't looking for no trouble. The boy just started messin' with me in first period, after the announcements. He heard my name mentioned and went off on me with bad names and stuff. I ignored him until he ran into me in the hallway."

His grandfather finally spoke: "I knew that wrestling stuff was trouble. Ain't been in that stuff a month and look at you – fightin' in school."

"Pop, it wasn't my fault. I didn't do anything to start it."

"Don't matter. Still in trouble. Get you off that team, that's the first thing that needs to be done."

"Mr. Hayes, if I can," Mr. Griffith interrupted, "I don't know if that is a good idea. I'm not here to tell you your business, but wrestling had nothing to do with this little scrape. I don't know if it is a good idea to take him off it. I hear he's pretty good, and those wrestlers are among the best kids in the school. He won't get into any trouble with that group. These are the exact people he *needs* to hang around."

"What about this fight? I mean, you can't be excusing fightin'. No excuse for that."

"Boys will be boys. It wasn't that big a deal. It wasn't gang-related. Jamal got the best of it, so I don't think there will be a rematch anytime soon. The other kid, Henry, is not that bad a kid, just wants to fit in. There are other ways we can deal with this problem in-house. Coach Russo and I can handle this situation just fine with a day or two of in-school-suspension and, I imagine that Coach Russo could come up with some extra push-ups and running at practice."

"He ain't goin' downtown? I thought he'd be taken to juvenile court for fighting. I read the papers. Schools ain't playin' with fightin' and stuff these days."

"I have a bit of say in that. We're a small school way out here in Frayser. The Board kind of leaves us to ourselves sometimes, gives me some discretion when it comes to things like jail. I really don't want to send two more young men to jail. Fighting is bad, but it's a fact of life with boys. You remember when we were kids. I fought all the time. In fact, the gym teacher had a pair of boxing gloves for the occasional fight between students. He forced them to fight. Can't do that any more, even though I'd love to do it."

"What about a suspension?" asked Mr. Hayes. "I can't see how he don't get suspended."

"As I said, I have some leeway when it comes to disciplinary matters. I can't see suspending him for a week or ten days for a little dust-up. He's a good kid, just took care of himself. I don't think you'd be against that."

"No, the boy got to stand up for himself. But he got in with the wrong folks in Chicago. It's why he's here. I don't want to see that mess repeated down here. Foot in his butt if it does. Both from you and me."

"I agree. I do believe, however, that this matter is small and can be handled by Coach Russo and me. No need to start a paper trail this early in his time here at Kennedy."

Jamal stayed silent throughout the entire conversation. Each time he tried to speak, his grandfather's stare told him to zip it. Mr. Griffith looked to him and asked, "What do you think of a few days of ISS instead of a ten day out of school suspension and a trip to the Board over on Hollywood?"

"Sounds a lot better," answered Jamal.

"ISS ain't no joke. No talking and nothing but class work from 7:15 until 2:15. You're like a prisoner. You stay with the same group all day, eat together, etc. Oh, and Coach Russo has a special practice for those wrestlers who end up in ISS. They don't usually like it, with all the push-ups and running. Price to pay though for getting put in ISS."

Jamal and his grandfather walked out of the office. Jamal didn't say a word, nor did his grandfather. When they were in the hallway outside the office, Mr. Hayes said. "Boy, I'll see you when you get home. Still don't know if you are gonna' keep up with that wrestling stuff. I don't like getting calls from the office when I'm at work. Makes me look bad, like I don't know how to raise a boy. You go to practice today. Tell the coach I'm thinking of putting you off the team. Okay?"

"Yes sir."

"Alright. I will see you at 6:30 or so when I pick you up."

"Yes sir," said Jamal. He waited a moment, and then added, "Pop, I don't want to quit the team. I really like it. I'll do some extra work at home if you want. I really want to stay on the wrestling team."

Lonny Hayes didn't answer right away. "I'll think about it." Then he walked out the school's back door to his truck, which was parked in the school's small lot.

• •

Coach Russo called practice to a start with a blow of his whistle. As the team gathered at his feet, he looked around the room. "Monday, boys. Where else would you rather be?" He didn't wait for an answer. His usual Monday inquiry. It was meant to measure the excitement and commitment of the team. If you could be excited on a Monday, you were hardcore and into wrestling. The sport was a six-day-a-week venture in high school. There was practice or matches Monday through Friday, and then tournaments on Saturday, leaving just Sundays off for the entire four month season. Wrestling was much different than football, in that football practiced Monday through Thursday, with a game on Friday. There were only ten football games, while there were up to 18 wrestling matches and tournaments every weekend between November and January. Football players got off Saturday and Sunday. Wrestlers had just one day off. The two sports' workouts were quite different also. Wrestling was more difficult for the body, with all the conditioning required. The dieting was another difference. Football coaches wanted players to bulk up, while in wrestling, most wrestlers needed to lose or maintain their weight. "Where else would you rather be" was Coach Russo's way of stating that the wrestlers were a bit more dedicated to their sport than football players or any of the other athletes at the school. *You had to be excited – even fanatical – to be a wrestler.*

"It is my understanding Jamal that you had a bit of trouble in the hallway today. Is that correct?" Russo asked. He already knew the answer. He just wanted to see if Jamal would admit it.

"Yes sir. Boy started something with me."

"Did you finish it?"

"Yes sir."

"Did you get your money's worth?"

"Yes, I think so."

"Good. I never want any of you guys to start a fight, but if someone lays their hands on you, I do expect you to be men. And take care of your business. If you do it right, and get your money's worth, you won't have any more problems. I guarantee it." He paused to let this sink in. "Now, you do owe me something Jamal. We'll get that done today. While the other guys practice, you will do push-ups and run. You will do duck walks with a weight bar over your shoulders. You will do physical things the entire three hours of practice. I'll be watching from the side, so don't slack off. I will see it."

Jamal didn't like the sound of things, especially the groans he heard from his teammates when Coach Russo mentioned the duck walks and "physical things." This could be bad.

"Let's go," said Coach Russo, as he blew his whistle, prompting the team to jump up and assume their spots for the start of practice: captains in the middle of the huge circle of wrestlers. This warm-up would be the last restful moment for Jamal. Three hours later, he would (literally) almost have to crawl out to his grandfather's truck.

First, there was the typical warming up with the team with all its push-ups and sit-ups. The usual six rounds of jump rope followed this with the exercises interspersed between each round. Then came the 45-pound bar and the duck walks across and around the mat. It hurt. Jamal took the bar and placed it across his shoulder blades, placing his hands on the bar to balance it. He then got into a deep squat, his knees bent and back straight. He was told to walk from this squat, which was very tough. It was tough to keep his balance. But he kept at it. If the first minute was difficult, the next twenty were impossibly tough. His thighs ached, as did his knees. After a lap of the mat, he was told to do twenty-five push-ups and 25 corkscrews. Then it was back to the bar and the duck walks. At one point, Coach Russo told Jamal to stop and stay in one place. He told him to stay in one place and hop with the bar over his shoulders. He hopped steadily for as long as the practice period lasted. While it was just three minutes, it seemed five. His thighs were telling him it had to be ten. After six rounds with the hopping, Coach Russo came over to Jamal. He was carrying what looked like a water hose. It wasn't; it was a jump rope, one that weighed six pounds. He gave Jamal the rope, telling him to get busy on the next period. Jamal struggled mightily with the heavy rope; it hit him in his own head several times. He couldn't seem to find the rhythm needed to get it over his head. Jumping with a fast rope was hard; this was murder. You wanted to jump it like the fast rope, but the rope's weight didn't allow you to do so. Most times the rope hit you in the back of the head, or you fell to the ground, your balance thrown off by the rope's weight.

At the water break, which typically indicated the half waypoint in practice, Jamal was beat. His legs throbbed from the duck walks and the rope. He wondered what was next in his "punishment." Coach Russo walked into the locker room and emerged with a pair of dumbbells in his hand. His punishment had arrived.

"Jamal, when we start back, the first thing you will do is lunges across the mat with these 25 pound dumbbells. You do just as we do at the start of practice, except you have one of these in each hand. Lunge all the way across – your knee touching the mat – and lunge all the back. Then you will stand in one place and do reverse lunges, stepping all the way back, your chest out."

Coach Russo demonstrated the backward lunge. He then gave the dumbbells to Jamal and blew the whistle for the second half of practice to begin. Jamal began his lunges across the mat. One time down and back had him dying; his thighs burned. After fifteen minutes of lunging his way across the mat, Coach Russo told him to begin the reverse lunges in one place. These were difficult to do. It seemed he could do one side well, but his other side, his left, he could not do so well, losing his balance as he tried to step back with his left leg. After a few attempts, he finally got the feel of it down and succeeded in doing a full set of twenty – ten on each side. "Two more sets, Jamal," Coach Russo said. The man could run the regular practice *and* keep an eye on him.

The next two sets took a long time to complete. His legs were gone. There was no strength or energy left in them. Jamal had to concentrate solely on each leg to get it to lunge forward. In twenty-five minutes, he was done, his legs jelly-like. Coach Russo, who was demonstrating a move for one of the other freshmen, saw him and came over to him.

"Legs burning?" he asked.

"Yes."

"Good. Your legs will be strong after today. Now, your next exercise is a clean and jerk with the dumbbell. You take in one hand" – he grabbed one of the barbells and demonstrated – "and you clean it up to your shoulder before you jerk it above your head. You do sets of twelve on each arm. Three of 'em. Get after it. Let me see you do one to see if you got it."

Jamal grabbed the dumbbell and held it at his beltline. He cleaned the weight up just as he had seen Coach Russo do, and then jerked it above his head. It didn't seem to be that tough.

"Good, that is just how you do it. Sets of twelve, three of 'em."

Jamal went to work. The exercise was not that difficult…the first five reps. Of course, it then got very tough. The last three reps on his right arm were agonizing. He then had to do the left side. Pain. By the time of his third set, he had great difficulty heaving the 25-pound dumbbell to his shoulder, much less above his head. His three sets took a good fifteen minutes to get done, not because he didn't try, but because he had little energy left. Coach Russo came over to him.

"Get 'em done?"

"Yes sir."

"Okay. Now we do three sets of shoulder presses with the dumbbells." He again grabbed the dumbbells and demonstrated, putting both dumbbells at his shoulder level and pressing them both above his head. "Very important to keep both even and on the same level as you go up. Works the shoulders real good. Get after it. Three sets of twelve."

Jamal went to work, the sweat pouring off him. He had not rested one second since practice had started. He was either duck-walking, jumping rope, lunging, cleaning a dumbbell or now, shoulder pressing these dumbbells. Pain and hurt.

At the conclusion of his third set, Coach Russo once again came over to Jamal and got him started on yet another exercise: dumbbell squats. "Grab each dumbbell in each hand, just like you did with the lunges, and squat. Make sure you keep your back straight and look up when you squat. Keep your feet a little wider than your shoulders. Deep squat. Make those thighs work. Let me see you do one."

Jamal grabbed the dumbbells and attempted to do one. Coach Russo corrected his form and made him do it again. "That's it. Just like that. Three sets of fifteen. Legs need more reps," he ordered as he went off to the rest of the team.

Just like the dumbbell cleans, this exercise didn't seem that tough at first. At first. It got much tougher the longer you did it. His thighs were already shot from the duck walk and hops earlier. These squats just added to the tightness and pain in his thighs. He labored mightily to get through the three sets. He would get to number ten okay, but then it seemed his legs would fight him on the last five, as if to ask, "Aren't these negotiable?"

When done with the dumbbell squats, Coach Russo walked towards Jamal with what looked like a small weight lifting bar. It was about half the size of a bench press bar and weighed less. Instead of 45 pounds, this smaller bar weighed twenty-five pounds. "Okay, Jamal, last thing today. You get to run while we finish up the regular practice. You will run around the practice gym. We got twenty-five minutes left. You can jog it, but you will run the entire time."

Doesn't sound too bad, thought Jamal, even if my legs are gone.

"One thing though. You have to carry this bar with you. Above your head, pushing it up and down, as you run."

Jamal knew there was a catch. There was no way Coach Russo was just going to let him lightly jog around the gym.

"Just push it up and down over your head as you jog around the gym. Here you go. Get after it. Don't slack up. I will be watching."

Jamal took the bar and started his jog. It took a second to get the rhythm of the running and the pressing of the bar above his head. Once he got settled into the run, it didn't take long for the pain to creep into it. This time the stiffness came from his shoulders, as well as his legs. Twenty-five minutes? He didn't know if he could go another two minutes, but he chugged along the best he could.

Just as his gait had lessened to a near-crawl, Jamal heard the final whistle and call of the day: "Shoot and leap! Jamal, you come on over and take part in this." Jamal cringed. Coach Russo would being him back to the team and let him participate in the one drill he (and the team) despised. Shoot and leap was the elementary leapfrog on steroids. It required quickness, agility and endurance to get through one minute rotation of the drill.

Jamal put the bar down and took his place among the team on the mat. He got a partner for the drill, taking his place in front of his partner, who was on one knee prepared to "shoot" through his open legs before "leapfrogging" back over Jamal's back to his start position, where he would repeat the movement. Jamal would count the reps his partner got for the time allotted.

Coach Russo blew the whistle, and the team began the drill. Some were far better than others. Bigger wresters had a tougher time with this drill than did the smaller guys. A 103 or 112 pounder could easily rip off 50 or more repetitions of the drill, while a 189 or 215 pound wrestler might be lucky to get 35 reps. Jamal and his partner – both 152 pounders – typically would hit somewhere in between 30 and 40 reps, meaning 40 shots through the legs with 40 leapfrogs over the back.

As Coach Russo counted down the final seconds of the first rotation, Jamal counted his partner's reps, encouraging him to keep working until the final whistle. "41-42—keep on pushing!" The whistle ended the first rotation. The second man had to match or exceed his partners total number of reps. Jamal's partner had gotten 42 repetitions. He'd have to get 43. Coach Russo made his way over to Jamal's side of the mat. "I'm gonna' watch Jamal here and make sure he gets his today. What's he got to get? 43? I'm watching Jamal."

The whistle blew, beginning the last rotation. Jamal, despite the stiffness in his legs, arms, and shoulders – his whole body – nonetheless pushed it to the max. "Thirty seconds. Halfway," yelled coach Russo. Jamal had thirty reps done at the half way mark. *Push it harder*, he told himself. *Don't think about the hurt.* He continued to hustle, to push. "38, Jamal. 39," his partner told him. "Keep it going, don't stop." Coach Russo started his countdown, "10-9-8-7…" causing each of the working wrestlers to up their pace. "…6-5-4-3-2-1!" Coach's whistle ended the drill. Wrestlers sprawled all over the mat, their breathing heavy. "How many did Jamal get?" asked Coach Russo. "If he didn't get the number, we do it again."

"46," answered Andrew, Jamal's practice partner.

"Good work, Jamal! Okay, boys, let's take it home. Cool it down."

The team circled up just like it did at the end of each day and began their daily ritual that ended practice: a big circle with the seniors in the middle. Twenty-five jumping jacks, followed by a big leap in the air to twenty-five push-ups on the ground followed by twenty-five crunches on their backs. Then it was back to the feet for fifteen of each. The last go-round would find the team counting down from ten the jumping jacks, push-ups and the crunches. The ritual would end with a circle of wrestlers with Coach Russo in the middle of the circle with any end of the day comments. Today, the comments were few, just a comment on the upcoming holiday schedule and one about a former wrestler who was on a college team. As the team worked its way to the locker room for the daily weigh-in, Coach Russo walked beside Jamal. "How you feel? Tight, stiff?"

"Yeah. Real tight," answered Jamal.

"It's still better than being suspended and out of school. You got one heck of a workout today. You also learned that fighting, while a last resort, should be avoided when possible. Such activity can lead to a sore night."

"I can tell. I still ain't letting no one run up on me."

"Walking away doesn't mean that. I fully expect you to defend yourself, but there has to be consequences, if for just the principal. The office usually suspends all involved in fighting. This is my way to keep you in school. Understand?"

"Yes sir."

Jamal weighed in at his lowest point the entire season: 146 pounds.

As he walked out the locker room door, Coach Russo told one of his varsity wrestlers, "We might have a little competition for you at 145 pounds this season. Jamal is right there with you."

Jamal just smiled as he left the locker room.

— Ten —

There was silence at the dinner table, as usual. Lonny didn't speak much, small talk not being his thing.

"I spoke with your mother today, Jamal. She called while you were at practice."

Jamal had not spoken with his mom in two weeks. Something about the rules of the place she was at. In his five weeks stay in Memphis, he had talked with her just five times, once a week, usually on Sunday. He did have, however, many letters from his mom. He got one or two a week. She, apparently, had plenty of free time to write. Jamal cherished those letters, though the frequency of them wore out his delight in getting them.

"How is she doing?" Jamal asked.

"Says she is doing real well. Told me to tell you hello, and that she'd try to catch you later in the week. She gets more calls now. Says she has earned them, whatever that means."

"I hate I missed her. She know when she will call again?"

"No, said she'd try to talk to you Sunday."

More silence followed. In a few minutes, the topic Jamal dreaded arose. "Jamal, I been thinking about this wrestling stuff. I think I'm taking you off the team. This fight you got into. I can't help but think it is a bad sign."

"Pop, you can't do that—"

"Boy, yes I can. You under this roof, and you'll do what I say—"

"—I didn't do anything wrong. I just defended myself. It wasn't my fault."

Lonny continued. "Don't interrupt me, boy. It ain't just the fight. This whole wrestling thing takes up too much time. Your chores suffer. I bet your grades ain't so good either. Part of the deal coming here was getting you right with school and back on track. I don't see how this wrestling stuff does that, just takes up all your time.

Jamal stayed silent before saying, "I knew you'd do this. Just knew it. It don't matter what I do. You never listen to me.

Lonny shot Jamal a look, one that usually indicated trouble. Or was it disbelief? Jamal didn't ever talk back to his grandfather. Ever.

Jamal continued: "Ever since I got here, you been on me." The "look" intensified. "From the first day, you been treating me like I done something wrong. No, a whole lot of wrong. It's like you hate me sometimes."

"Is that what you think, boy?" The "look" disappeared, replaced with a shaking head. "Damn. Young folks. That's the problem with being young. Think you know every damn thing, yet don't know nothing."

"What am I supposed to think?" More shaking of the head. "You always on me. I can't seem to do anything right. If you say anything nice to me, I know it's just a matter of time before you on me again. You used to be nice, like my buddy—"

"I ain't ever gonna' be your buddy. And before you moved in here, you was my grandson, and I treated you like that. But since November, you my responsibility. It changes things, changes everything."

"I don't know why things have to change. I am still the same."

"I don't think you are. That stuff in Chicago didn't 'just' happen. You did do it. You did hang out with some fools. I heard all about them. Don't tell me you the same 'cause when you got here, you weren't. None of that mess that happened up north gonna' happen down here. Not at all. I ain't going through all that again."

"Again?" Jamal asked. "What you mean 'again?'"

"Nothing. Wrestling is done. That's it." That "look" again.

"Pop, you did mean something about 'again.'"

Silence.

"Pop, I just got here. You ain't never been through anything with me. What you mean 'again?'" Curiosity.

"Nothing boy. Ain't no matter now any how."

He's hiding something, Jamal thought. Pry a little further. "I don't see how there can be an 'again,' Pop. I got here just a few months ago, and I ain't done nothing since I been here except school, wrestling, and church. I also done stuff for you. I don't get 'again.'"

"It's your mom, if you must know. I didn't do right by her, and I won't make those same mistakes twice. Man don't get second chances at family stuff often. I ain't making the same mistake with you."

"What mistake?" asked Jamal.

"Not being there. Always working. Not paying attention to everything. If I'd have done better, she might not have the problems she do now."

Jamal was taken back to a chat with his mom some time back. "Mom don't feel that way. She told me the opposite, that if she'd paid more attention to you, then she'd be in a lot better shape. She blames everything on herself."

"She's wrong on that one. I coulda' kept her straight and away from—"

Jamal finished his sentence: "—my father."

"Yeah, him. The more I think, the more I believe that there is something I coulda' done to stop that. But I didn't see it then, and your momma paid the price. You paying the price too."

"I don't know what you mean by me 'paying' too."

"Simple. You down here with me, and you ain't where you need to be – with your mom. All because of him. Your mom don't meet that bum, and she ain't got no problems."

"You mean, like me?" A hurt look took over Jamal's face.

"Heck no, boy! I mean problems like the ones that got her in the shape she in. That man destroyed my little girl. She was on the right path, and then she met him. It ruined her. Took all the life out of her. Living with a bum will do that to you. That fool robbed my little girl of the best years of her life. She ain't been the same since. He was the worst thing ever did happen to her."

Jamal was confused now. If his grandfather thought meeting Marvin Worth was the worst thing that ever happened to his daughter, then what did he think of Jamal, the result of their pairing?

"I guess I see why you don't like me so much some time. My daddy." More hurt on the face.

"Don't like? More of that young folks stupidity coming out. That's crazy, boy. If anything, you are the only good thing that man ever did, even if he didn't mean to do it. What I mean is that your daddy didn't ever start out to do anything good. You happened, but it was in spite of your daddy. He was not a good man then. From what I hear, he ain't gotten any better. In prison, for killing someone. You are his son, and you do favor him, but that is where it all ends. You ain't nothing like him and ain't gonna' be anything like him. If I thought you were anything like him, you wouldn't be here."

"I never knew him. I only know what I heard about him, and none of it's good. I won't be anything like him."

"Which is where I come in. You, whether you know it or not, were headed right down the path he was. It is why I have been tough on you. Something happened to your daddy. Who knows what. Maybe a fight one day at school. Who knows? He was a good athlete and all. Coulda' had it all. Did have it all. And threw it all away." Pause for emphasis. "That carjacking you was involved with in Chicago –"

"It wasn't a carjacking, Pop," Jamal interrupted.

"Whatever it was, it wasn't a good thing. Who's to say that if you hadn't got caught that you wouldn't have just kept on doing what you were doing. You might have been there with your buddies. They headed for trouble. You might not have had the chance to go to prison like your daddy; you might have just gone to the graveyard. It's why I think that fight at school is so bad, that is some sort of sign for me. One I need to notice."

"I already told you I just defended myself. I ain't no hoodlum or thug. I ain't my daddy, and I don't plan on being like him either."

"That boy you got into it with, he coulda' got hurt. I saw him. You did a number on him. That wrestling stuff taught you how to do that. Bad sign to me: a sport showing you how to damage folks. Might make you think you can solve all your problems with that stuff."

"Wrestling didn't have anything to do with that fight. That boy had been messing with me for weeks. Maybe it was because I was new. I don't know. I just know it wasn't wrestling that caused it. All I did was take up for myself, just like you'd have done. I'd have done that without wrestling. Wrestling just showed how to take care of myself well. That boy won't mess with me anymore."

Jamal continued defending himself. Unusual territory in his grandfather's house. But he felt confident. He and his grandfather were actually talking to each other instead of him listening to his grandfather talk: "Wrestling has been the best thing to happen to me. You said my grades are bad. Well, they aren't. I almost got all my grades back up to where they used to be. I got all A's except for two classes, and I am working on getting those up. My schoolwork has improved because of wrestling. I have to get to wrestle. Because of wrestling, I like going to school. I look forward to it. I like being on the team. I don't know. It's hard to explain. I've never felt this way about anything. I just know that the idea of not wrestling makes me feel awful. I'd miss it like crazy, and I can't help but think my schoolwork and everything would suffer. School just wouldn't be the same. I wouldn't have the friends I have. It's hard to explain."

Pop mused. "Well, this is true. Ain't no boy of mine gonna' let someone walk on him." More musing. "If what all you say is true, then I'll give this thing more thought. But I ain't promising nothing. Fighting at school ain't right, especially these days with all the young folks in gangs and stuff. You never know if three or four aren't going to jump you."

Jamal agreed. "There are a lot of bad folks out there. But don't you see, wrestling is where all the good guys are. They graduate. They go to college. They get good jobs. Coach Russo got guys he used to coach who come by all the time. Some of 'em in suits and got good jobs. I want to be like that. I don't want to be hanging out on the streets and stuff. I don't know if I thought about stuff like that before wrestling."

Pop resumed his usual look, a semi-frown. He then spoke: "I won't apologize for being hard on you. It's my job. If only more boys these days had someone like me, then we wouldn't have all the problems we got now with young folks killing each other and in jail. It's my job to help make you a man. It's serious business, and I don't shy away from it. You can bet that I will watch you like a hawk and make you do right. And I'm gonna' put a foot in your butt when you need it." He stopped and stared at Jamal. "And it don't matter how many 'rasslin' moves they teach you. I can still take you." A smile crept onto Pop's face.

"Pop, I really don't want to quit wrestling. Please, let me continue. Coach says I got a real good chance at winning the city tournament.

I'd like to try. You gonna' do whatever you think best, but give me this. Wrestling is the first thing in my life I ever done on my own. I'm in the best shape of my life. I am busy everyday. My grades and conduct are good. The school's principal and my teachers all say that I am doing good. I'm home at night. Heck, I been so busy with wrestling and school that I wouldn't know where to go in the neighborhood to get into trouble, even if that is what I wanted to do. Wrestling actually helps your job. It keeps me in line. Because of it, I only know three places in Memphis: school, church and home. And I like it that way. Please, let me stay on the team."

The stare softened. He didn't speak right away. "Well, you do go to sleep early every night. You are on a diet, so you ain't running up the grocery bill." Jamal smiled. "I guess pulling you off the team wouldn't be so good. You can stay on the team, but I am going to ground you. Coach Russo punished boys for misbehavior at school. I got to do the same. You are grounded for a week. One week. For the fight. That's it. No practice, no TV. Just school, chores and church. That's it. I'll call coach tonight and tell him."

Jamal realized that this was the best deal he was going to get, so he just replied, "Yes sir."

Before he left the room, Pop turned to Jamal and said, "Hating you? Boy, you must be out of your mind. I don't care who your daddy is. There is no way I could hate you. While half of him might be in you, the *better* half come from me. I couldn't hate you if I tried. I see you, and I see my little girl, your mom. I see me. I see your grandmother, bless her soul. I couldn't hate you if I wanted to. I see you get up in the morning, and it makes me want to get up and do more to make life better for you. I see you doing your schoolwork at the computer, and I see a future doctor or businessman. Heck, I even maybe the future President. When I see you win on that mat, I feel as good as you do, maybe even better. This'll sound weird, but each day when you arise, I am reborn. It all gives me a reason to keep on getting up every day. Since I lost your grandmother, I ain't felt like that much. Not since you got here. Now I look forward to each day and even the future. I want to live a long time, long enough to see you have kids and to see them do well. As long as you here, I got a reason to keep on going, and I like that. I take that serious and don't you forget it."

Pop didn't do emotion well. A pat on the back or the top of the head was the full extent of his "physical emotion." He *never* talked feelings or emotions, keeping everything locked deep inside. The strong, silent type, like John Wayne, one of his old favorite movie stars.

His words still hanging in the air, Pop left the room for his own bedroom.

Grounded for a week. I can handle it, thought Jamal, as he sat on his bed and opened up his copy of George Orwell's *Animal Farm.* Time to catch up with Napoleon and the other animals on the former Manor Farm.

— Eleven —

Jamal's grounding came at the best time for him, as far as wrestling went. It was the week heading into the holidays, and there was only one match on the schedule. He would miss that one and that week of practice. The Christmas break would start on Friday. He'd miss the rest of this week and the first Monday of the break. I can handle it.

Being grounded by his grandfather though would prove to be, in a word, hell. Jamal had heard other boys speak of being grounded. In his elementary days, his mom Anna had grounded him. But it never stuck. A week of restrictions would actually turn into two or three days tops. Moms can be such a soft touch.

Not true with Pop.

The morning of his first day of restrictions, Pop laid it all out for Jamal. "Boy, you get out of school at 2:15. I will call this house at 3 PM. Answer that phone before the third ring. When you do, I will tell you where your list of chores is. You get it and get it done. When I get home, I will check and see if it is all done right.

"If you don't answer by the third ring, I'll add a day to your punishment. If the answering machine picks up the phone, I will add another week to it. So you better get home right after school. I talked to Coach Russo last night. He knows and agrees with me. He also gave me a list of things for you to do when you are done with your chores. Exercises and stuff. Said you would know what they were. Told me to tell you to drop by and get a rope from him. He said the workout he got for you will keep your wind up and your weight down. Understand?"

Jamal nodded his head. If only he knew.

Like most teens, he just knew that Pop would soften on the grounding and let up a day or two early. Not happening with Lonny Hayes.

Every day, Jamal hurried home to catch the phone and receive his marching orders, which included every sort of chore imaginable that can be done during the winter months: raking and bagging leaves, cleaning out gutters, rearranging the garage (again), cleaning the windows and screens. When he was done with his grandfather's house, he was told to go next door and help Mrs. Johnson with her yard. Like Tao in the Clint Eastwood film Gran Torino, Pop shopped his grandson around the neighborhood to neighbors in need of yard work. He even had Jamal go to an old graveyard down the road and clean a lot of it up. "Pop, this ain't our yard," he said emphatically, only to have Pop say, "Those folks don't need to be in dirty place like that. You might be there one day, and you'd want someone to clean it up too." Then there was Coach Russo's routine each night at the end of the afternoon's labor: 100 push-ups, 100 crunches, six rounds of jump rope, 100 deep knee bends. And Pop made him do that too, often acting the coach in the garage with Jamal. "Push it, boy. That ain't working that rope!" He once even took the jump rope himself and showed Jamal that he "still had it," jumping the rope and crossing it in front of him. Jamal was glad when the week was up.

Holidays were for the regular students at Kennedy. They were non-existent for the Kennedy wrestlers. Over the two-week break, they would get exactly four days off – Christmas Eve, Christmas Day, New Year's Eve and New Year's Day. The varsity team didn't get this, as they had to practice Christmas night. They were leaving for a tournament on the day after Christmas. Weight had to be right for the tourney, as they would get little practice time after they arrived in Chattanooga. The freshmen and JV guys had three matches in one day against three other schools at Collierville High School, a huge school in Collierville, a town outside of Memphis. Coach Russo had no life it seemed. During wrestling season, all he did was wrestling-related stuff: practice, varsity matches, freshmen and JV events, tournaments for all levels. He even had many of the older guys working at FedEx Forum raising money over the Thanksgiving weekend. Of course, he spent all spring and summer with the team raising money in all sorts of ways, mostly at AutoZone Park selling food for the Memphis Redbirds, the city's AAA baseball team. It worked. The Kennedy wrestlers always rode in buses to matches, and the team had two out of town trips. While the JV and freshmen guys got the older singlets and warm-ups, the varsity team had brand new stuff that looked as good as the stuff the private schools wore.

School ended on a Friday, a full week ahead of Christmas. The JV and freshmen team had the meet at Collierville on the following Wednesday. Monday and Tuesday's practices were an odd mix of wrestling, weights and basketball. Jamal would only get to Tuesday's practice due to this punishment, something he hoped he didn't ever have to go through again. Prison was not that tough.

Coach mixed it up over the holidays. Sure, the practices were three hours long, but they were not the same routine, so both days were fun. The quad-match at Collierville was set to start at 10:00 AM with weigh-ins at 9:00 AM. The team met at Kennedy at 7:30 AM, so that they'd be able to check weight and make the hour long drive to Collierville, making sure they arrived fifteen minutes early – "Coach Russo time" – for the weigh-in. The three other teams were arriving as the Kennedy bus pulled up to the Collierville High parking lot. Collierville, St. Ignatius, and North

High School were competing with Kennedy today. North was here, which meant for Jamal that Colin kid, the real good kid who had beaten him at St. Paul a couple of weeks earlier. *I hope I don't have to wrestle him first,* thought Jamal.

The teams weighed in and were on the two mats warming up. Coach Russo was in the hospitality room with the other coaches getting the order for the day. All teams would get three dual matches for the day, which meant, minus forfeits, each wrestler would get three matches for the day. As the team warmed up, Jamal looked around the gym. Nice. Collierville was a public high school, but their facilities looked like those of St. Paul's. Haves and have nots again. He recognized some of the wrestlers on the other teams from the tournament at St. Paul. Coach Russo had told the team that if someone had beaten them to take their name down because they might see them again soon. *Colin Young, hello again.*

Kennedy had St. Ignatius first, and they routed them, winning ten of fourteen matches. St. Ignatius won four matches – two by forfeit, one by pin and one by decision. A pin, or "fall" as it is formally known—holding your opponent's shoulders down for a two count – is worth six team points, while a decision – a match that goes the entire six minutes can get a team anywhere between three and five points, depending on the margin of victory. Kennedy beat St. Ignatius 57-21. Considering they got 12 points by forfeit, it was a complete rout. Jamal pinned his opponent in the first period. He handled him easily throughout the minute and a half they were on the mat. Most of the Kennedy wrestlers won easily.

Kennedy faced Collierville next. They were a tougher group, but Kennedy still managed to beat them with ease, winning nine of fourteen matches. Most of the matches ended with decisions, the final score being 36-15. Jamal defeated his opponent 14-12 in a wild match that managed to touch every corner of the mat. The kid was strong as a mule, and Jamal couldn't hold him down. He had him on his back two or three times, only to have the kid literally bench press him off. The kid had put Jamal on his back too, but Jamal managed to roll him over every time. With ten seconds in the match, and both boys on their feet, Jamal hit a double leg takedown and managed to hold his Catholic opponent down long enough to ride out the clock and win the match.

Colin Young up next.

The Kennedy team was 2-0 for the day, as was the North High Commandoes. The first round of matches had started with the 135-pound weight-class, while the second round began with the next weight class, 140 pounds. Wrestling dual events were done in this manner, Jamal had learned. At the beginning of a dual meet, the coaches meet with the referee in the locker room or at the head table to draw a weight class from a bag. All fourteen weight-classes are on little chips. If a coach draws the chip with "189" on it, the match begins at 189 pounds and works it way around back to "171," which would be the last match. It made no sense at all to Jamal. Just start with the small guys and go to the big guys. Simple. But what did he know? He was a wrestler with exactly one month of experience.

For the North match, Jamal would wrestle third. Colin and he began warming up the moment the 140-pound wrestlers ran out to the mat's center circle. While Jamal occasionally looked in the direction of Young, the North wrestler never looked in Jamal's direction. No need to be nervous or anxious over an opponent you pinned easily one month earlier.

The Kennedy team won the first two matches by decision. Kennedy 6 North 0. Jamal's turn now. Before he went to the head table to check in, Coach Russo pulled him close and said, "The last time you went against this kid, he beat you good. That was a month ago. You are much better now. Start fast and stay on top of him. Be aggressive from the first whistle. Get a tight and low stance. Hit the low single, the move we worked on two days ago. I remember you doing that move well. He'll never expect it."

Coach Russo was right. The low single leg takedown coach showed the team at practice was one of Jamal's favorites. He spent the rest of that practice getting his teammates with the move, even some of the upper-classmen. He could hit that move with the best of them.

The two wrestlers jogged to the center circle. The referee was at the head table, checking with the scorekeepers to make sure the right weight class and people were on the mat. He then paced to the center circle, told the wrestlers to shake hands and blew his whistle. Jamal struck first.

Crouched in a lower than usual stance, Jamal's lead foot, his right, was on the green line, lined up perfectly with Young's left foot, which was set on the red line. At the sound of the whistle, Jamal, whose stance was lower than the taller Young's, dropped to the mat, his right knee and elbow hitting the mat at the same time. His right hand cupped the heel of Young, while his left leg circled counterclockwise, providing leverage for the takedown. Three seconds into the match, and Jamal was leading 2-0. Colin was taken by surprise with the quick takedown. He had no time to counter it, so he bailed and went to his stomach and began to work to his base. Jamal was in control behind Young, his right arm tightly wrapped around his waist, his left hand on Young's left elbow. When Young went to move, Jamal would chop the left elbow and use his right arm to tilt him to his left shoulder. After two or three of the tilts, Young stood to his feet, with Jamal following him, both his hands wrapped tightly around his waist. The North wrestler began to fight the hands holding him, trying to tear them free. Jamal simply lifted Young into the air and took him back to the ground. *Waist, chop, tilt, thought Jamal.* Colin Young again stood up, and this time, he was able to tear himself free from Jamal's grip. "One point escape," said the referee, as he signaled it to the scorer's table. The two wrestlers circled each other, Jamal body-faking and changing his level. Colin Young was much more attentive than at match's start. He was not in that tall stance. He was now in a tighter, lower stance and pressed

Jamal, moving forward, tapping Jamal on his forehead. *He is fixing to take a leg shot, thought Jamal.* Correct. Young tapped Jamal on his forehead, and immediately he stepped right, his right foot outside of Jamal's left foot, his right arm wrapped around Jamal's lower leg, which he lifted into the air. Jamal couldn't keep his balance and fell to the mat. "Two points takedown," the referee said. The score was 3-2 in favor of Young. Jamal went to this feet and tore free. His quickness caught Young by surprise. "One point escape." As the two wrestlers circled each other, the time in the first period winded down—0:03, 0:02, 0:01. The referee blew his whistle, ending the first period. The match was tied 3-3. In their first match, Jamal didn't make it out of the first period. He was dominated and didn't even score a point, getting pinned quickly. What a difference four weeks made.

"Your choice green," said the referee, signaling to Jamal. Jamal looked to Coach Russo. Russo held his thumb down, signaling to Jamal to take the down position. In wrestling, the bottom position offers more chances to score. A wrestler can stand up and get one point for an escape and a try at a two-point takedown, or he can use a switch or some sit-out combination to score a two-point reversal. Jamal wasn't very good in the bottom position, so he would stand up and get back to the neutral. When he went to get set in the bottom position, he was already thinking of the takedown he would try when he got to his feet. "Set?" asked the referee. Jamal nodded yes. The referee signaled to Young to assume his position on top. Once set, the ref blew his whistle, signaling the start of the second period. Jamal went to his feet immediately and tore free, his quickness once again catching Young off-guard.

The two wrestlers were on their feet, moving around each other, each feinting at the other. The two locked up with each other; they each had a collar and elbow tie, moving each other around the middle circle. Jamal snapped down Young's head with his right hand, while he pulled his right arm, trying to position him for an attack. Jamal wanted to snap his head down and get him to rise up so he could double leg tackle him, but Young would have none of it. He was certain Young was doing the same thing – working a set up of a sort. He just didn't know what. Then he found out. "Two, takedown," signaled the referee. Jamal had stepped right into a fireman's carry and found himself perilously close to his back. He bellied down and tried to work himself to his hands and knees. Young was strong and experienced. While Jamal had been a wrestler for just a month, Young had probably been doing it since his middle school years. That was at the least two years experience. Of course, if he'd been wrestling six weeks, that would have been longer than Jamal.

Jamal worked himself to his hands and knees. He stood to his feet, only to be tripped back down. He then tried to work something on the mat, performing a sit-out and turn. Young simply followed him. No change in position. No score. He then stood to his feet again, fighting Young's hands off him. He was taken back to the mat by Young, which prompted another stand. This time it worked: Jamal was free. "One point escape," said the referee. The score was 5-4 in favor of Young. Jamal had to get this takedown. There was under a minute left in the second period. He wasn't tying up again with his more experienced opponent. That had been disastrous a minute earlier. No, he would stay on his feet, use movement and his quickness to create an angle of attack. Maybe the low single again. While not tying up with Young, Jamal did work his head, snapping it down and pushing it, trying to get his hips up to hit a double leg takedown. If he could get Young to reach at him, he'd take a shot. Then he did. Jamal had body-faked Young, causing him to reach at him, a little off balance. Jamal hit the double, dropping his level and attacking Young's legs, his shoulder in his hips. He lifted Young into the air and took him down to his back. And squeezed. While Young scrambled and moved to get off his back, Jamal squeezed like crazy. He couldn't hold him still, but he had him on his back. Jamal saw the clock at the scorer's table. There were just :15 seconds and counting left in the second period. He had to hold his position a little tighter. He moved his body – "t-ed up," Coach Russo called it – where it and Young's made a human "T." It would increase the leverage and the likelihood of a pin, as well as keep his opponent's legs from tangling up with his. Just five seconds left. More strength needed.

The referee blew his whistle and ended the period. The referee signaled to the table and said, "Three points nearfall." Jamal looked at the scoreboard. With his taken and nearfall points, he now led Young 9-5. His big move had netted him a five-point swing. Two minutes to go. Could he hold the lead?

It was Young's choice this last period. He chose down. The referee signaled to the North wrestler to take his place in the center circle, and then told Jamal to take the top position. Coach Russo yelled, "First move," which was something he often said in practice to get guys to thinking of their first movement once the whistle blew. Jamal was already thinking a spiral ride. He needed to do something to break Young down and ride him out for two minutes. If he could just get him on his back again, he knew he could pin him. While he knew just a few moves on top, Jamal knew the spiral and chop and tilt well. Outside of a half-nelson, he didn't know much about turning an opponent onto his back, but he knew that one move well. If he saw an opportunity, he'd run the half.

The whistle blew. Jamal never got the chance for the spiral or the chop. He never had a chance to think. His opponent was one step ahead of him, hitting a perfect switch, a hard switch, in fact. Jamal's shoulder hurt where the pressure of his own grip on Young's stomach had caused the reversal to use his own strength against him. It was now a one-point match. Jamal worked to his hands and knees and attempted his own switch, a move Coach Russo had reviewed with all the new guys in practice just this week. He didn't do it correctly. He knew because he was now on his back with Young squeezing the daylights – and breath – out of him. When he went to free his right arm and short-sit, he didn't get his arm totally free, nor did he get to his sit. He was extended and Young simple sucked him to his back.

The referee signaled back points as Jamal struggled to get free. No use. The referee blew the whistle. Jamal had been pinned. He was disappointed, even angry. While he didn't display any unsportsmanlike behavior, he was not overly sportsmanlike either. He shook his opponent's hand, walked to the North side of the mat and shook the coach's hand and then walked to the locker room, leaving his teammates behind on the benches. He just wanted to be alone. For just a moment. Coach Russo let him go. He knew exactly what was going on Jamal's head. A few minutes alone wouldn't hurt anything; it would likely help.

Jamal was more angry than disappointed. Angry at himself. Angry that he didn't pin Young when he had him on his back. What made him angriest was not that he had lost to Colin Young again, but that he *knew* he could beat him. Jamal knew that he didn't give it his best. Well, he didn't give it his best for six minutes. For the first two periods, Jamal was even with his more experienced rival. It was the last period. The mistaken effort at a switch. Coach Russo's words from earlier in the week came back to him: "*Stay with what you know. Don't try new stuff until you've mastered them at practice.*" I will remember that from now on, he thought. Jamal's thoughts went back to his first tournament and Coach Russo's comments on the bus before leaving the St. Paul parking lot: "You guys who lost a match or two today, remember it. This is a long season, and you may see those guys again. Beat them next time. Learn from your mistakes and keep on moving forward. Wrestling is a process, one that takes the entirety of the season to measure. Don't measure yourself by one or two matches or even one tournament. Wait until February to see where you are compared to where you were in November." Jamal could do that now. Colin Young had pinned him with ease just a few weeks before today. While he had pinned Jamal again today, he didn't do it so easily. He had to work for it. Frankly, Jamal thought he should have won the match in the second period. If he knew a little more about pinning his opponent, then he would have won. *A process...yes it is.*

The Kennedy-North match went down to the last match at 135 pounds. Kennedy was down 34-30. They needed Andrew Hunter, their freshman 135 pounder, to win by pin or technical fall to get the victory. It was a heck of a match. Both wrestlers knew that a win was at stake, and they left it all on the mat. In the end, the North wrestler avoided being the goat for the day, losing a 15-10 decision to Anthony. Coach Russo worked the referees the entire match, calling for the refs to call stalling on the North wrestler who repeatedly went backward or to call the pin. Anthony had his opponent on his back three times, and no whistle came. No matter how hard he pressed or squeezed, the North wrestler wouldn't be pinned; he always managed to get out of bounds or keep one shoulder up the slightest bit. Kennedy lost to North 34-33. It was pretty exciting, Jamal thought. His thoughts soon turned to his match. If he had won, then his team would have won. This didn't make him feel any better. Never mind that any other Kennedy wrestler who lost could say the same thing. Jamal just knew it was his fault. Of course, he didn't say anything. He kept his head low, hoping no one would notice him and be reminded of this fact. It never happened. Wrestling was not like that. Odd. In his old neighborhood, if someone blew a game or cost a team, even in a neighborhood game, someone would pay with taunts or checks from his teammates. Not happening here.

The teams lined up across from each other and walked towards each other, shaking their opponent's hands and congratulating them on the effort. When Jamal passed and shook hands with Colin Young, he almost told him, "I'll get you next time," but he didn't say it. Coach Russo wouldn't approve. Instead, it was Colin who spoke: "Man, you done got tough in a few weeks. You almost had me out there. See you at the city. It might be us in the finals."

Jamal answered: "I hope it is."

The Kennedy team finished the day 2-1. It was a good day, Coach Russo said on the bus. "We'll get 'em next time. That's what is great about wrestling. There's always a next time."

At the school, parents were waiting in the parking lot. Jamal's grandfather was not there. Coach Russo told Jamal to call his grandfather and tell him that he'd drop him off and not to come to the school. He let Jamal use his cell phone.

The ride home was short. Coach Russo did all the talking. "That was a heck of a match with the North kid."

"I lost," said Jamal.

"Yeah, but you can beat him. I know it. Remember the last match. It wasn't even a match, yet today, you gave him all he wanted. It just shows you how much you have improved. Believe me, you're in his head now. The Freshman City Championships should be fun to watch. I think you can beat him. What better place and time to do it than at the City Championships?"

"When are they?"

"The end of January. One month away. If you have improved this much in one month, what are you going to be like in another four weeks?" Jamal said nothing. "A lot. I know I can beat that kid."

Coach agreed. A silent moment. "I had a good chat with your grandfather last week before we got out of school. I wanted to check up on you and see how the grounding was going. He said things were good, that you were right on top of everything he had laid out for you. It was a good chat. I think he wants to see you do well. He's proud of what you're doing. He told me."

"He didn't say anything to me about it. Said he was gonna' talk with you, but he didn't say when he'd meet with you."

"We did it the Wednesday before the last Friday of school. He came by during the school hours. Spoke with the principal and me. We talked for over an hour. I don't think you have to worry about being taken off the team. Mr. Griffith told him how well you have adjusted and all. He told him how well you are doing in class and stuff. Your grandfather seemed pleased. He thinks the wrestling is a good thing. Just the impression I got."

"You don't know him. He's hard to predict. Never changes his expression."

"It's called a 'poker face.' Keeps people wondering what you are thinking."

"It's worked on me. I can't tell when he's in a good mood or bad. I just stay quiet and take care of my business."

"I think that's what he wants for you. Your grandfather is a good man. I have only met him a time or two, but he truly cares about you. I don't know what happened with you in Chicago, but it is on his mind. He doesn't want that same trouble to follow you down here. Truth be known, more kids in this neighborhood need a man like your grandfather."

"That's what he said. I'm doing my best. I'm doing good in school—"

"Well, 'doing well' in school," interrupted Coach Russo.

"Well, I am doing well in school. I'm not doing anything wrong. The only people I associate with are the team. Wrestling is all I do. I don't go out in the neighborhood much. Don't know any of the kids in the neighborhood. I stay home when we aren't practicing or at a tournament. I love wrestling. It's the first sport I have ever done, and I like it. The guys on the team are all good guys too. None of them are in trouble. I don't want to leave it. Pop told me he might take me off it. Said he was gonna' think it over."

"I don't think your wrestling days are over. I think he is using that threat to keep you scared and in line. In fact, I believe your wrestling is just beginning. Your grandfather and I had a great talk. I think he is on my side. But understand where he is coming from. He is right. He only wants the best for you. He doesn't want the trouble for you that so many young men are getting into. I am on his side there. If your grades slip, or if you get into any trouble at school, I am with him: you need to be off the team. The pressure is on you. Do right, and all will be okay.

"Do wrong, and you're off the team."

He paused for a moment to let those words sink in. "However, I don't see that happening. You have done a great job thus far. If there are issues at school, don't hesitate to come to me. I am more than your coach. My job is get you on down the road, graduating and all that, and in the process, make you one heck of a wrestler. It's all a process, just like wrestling. It's all connected – school, home, wrestling, family. All of it. Keep it all together. Let one part slip, and all of it suffers. It's tough, but it can be done. People do it every day. Life, it's just like my one rule: 'Show up every day.' Do your best every single day, and you'll be fine."

"Yes sir. Where was I when Pop came by?"

"You were in class. It didn't concern you. We got it all worked out. You just keep up your end of things." The car pulled up in front of Lonny's house. "You go in and get some rest. Enjoy the holidays. One of the guys will contact you about the holiday practices. You guys are gonna' get a couple of days work in before the new year. Then it is January, the tough part of the schedule."

"Yes sir. You have a Merry Christmas. Good luck with the team in Chattanooga," said Jamal, as he gathered his stuff together.

"You too. Great job out there today. Let's win the City in January."

"Yes sir. I want to get that Colin kid again."

"You will. You will. Enjoy your break."

"Okay, coach. See you next year."

"Not if I see you first."

Jamal laughed slightly at the old joke. He shut the car door and headed toward the front door of Pop's house. It was still "Pop's house," not "his" house. Maybe some day soon, he'd have "his" house, one like it should be – his Mom back and things back to like they were supposed to be.

— Twelve —

The holidays were odd. Jamal felt out of place. It was his first Christmas without his mother. Lonny was hard to judge. His mood varied little. It seemed to teeter between angry and angriest most of the time, his face especially. Jamal could not remember when he saw his grandfather smile. Did he ever? Not since Jamal's arrival. *Poker face.* Maybe coach was right. Pop didn't want people to know what he was thinking. Beneath the seeming permanent scowl, maybe, just maybe, a smile lurked. Maybe.

He wondered why his grandfather didn't tell him of meeting with Coach Russo and the principal. The meeting happened last week, and not one word about it. Maybe he would get to keep wrestling. In the meantime, there were chores. Many chores. Jamal never knew there could be so much to be done in a yard during the wintertime, but there was, or so Pop made it seem It was as if the leaves didn't get raked, bagged and set by the curb, the whole world would end – or at least, Jamal's would. One day it was the yard, the next it would be organizing the garage. How could so much stuff get crammed into such a small garage? Of course, none of it was tossed aside, just reorganized. It was a, Jamal guessed, a neater mess now.

No matter how long Lonny lived, there was no way he would ever use all the tools in that garage.

The last two or three Christmases had not been good for Jamal. Anna's problems destroyed the holidays. Sure, he'd get a gift or two, but that was not what Jamal liked about the holidays of his boyhood. He enjoyed the *feel* of family. When he was a little boy, his mom and he would trek to Memphis to Lonny's house. The mood was always happy and festive, with distant relatives filling the house with happiness and, especially, great and plentiful food. Jamal was just a little boy at the time, but he loved to stuff himself with the turkey and all the trimmings. And the desserts! He especially loved his Aunt Della's – his late grandmother's sister – sweet potato pie. Thanksgiving and Christmas were the only two dates he ever ate this wonderful delectable, and he so looked forward to the dates. Even Lonny was in great spirits those days. Or was it full of *spirits?* His late grandmother's family still came to Lonny's for Christmas in those years. Her brothers could always get Pop into a good mood. They talked of their youth and all the things they did. It was fun for Jamal to sit and listen to the past exploits of his grandfather. The man must have been something because the stories were never-ending.

Anna and Jamal had not been to Memphis for the holidays in some time. How could it be the same as he remembered?

On the day before Christmas Eve, Lonny took Jamal to the barbershop on Thomas and told the barber, an old friend of his apparently, to cut Jamal's hair. "High and tight!" he ordered "Melvin," his old friend. "Get him lookin' respectable. Got some folks comin' in town." This was news to Jamal. Pop hadn't said much in the previous days. He thought it would be just the two of them. He would be surprised.

On the morning of Christmas Eve, the first of the crew arrived: his Aunt Della and Uncle Wilson. He hadn't seen them in years, since the last Christmas he and Anna had come to Pop's for the holidays. Most of

Lonny's kinfolk had passed on; he was the last one. Only a long lost brother was left, but he hadn't been around in years, and Pop didn't expect to see him ever again. Nary a word was ever mentioned about one Mitchell Hayes. A falling out years ago. Time, distance and animosity prevented any sort of reunion. Jamal guessed it was the anger and not the distance that kept the two apart.

Aunt Della was the same as Jamal had remembered her: a large woman with huge pocketbook and a wonderful smile. She, he remembered, used to grab him a bear hug that literally smothered his small frame. When she entered the front door, she reverted to form and grabbed him, attempting to smother him again. Being ten years older and some pounds heavier, it was a tougher task, but one she attempted without hesitation. "Get over here boy, and give your Aunt Della a hug. Been such a long time." Outside of looking a little older, Aunt Della was just as Jamal remembered her. His Uncle Wilson, a tall and lean figure, was more like Lonny—not much of a talker. "Damn, let the boy breathe Della," he said. He shook hands with Jamal, once his aunt let go of him. Lonny sat and watched it all, getting their bags in the house, including some presents that were gift-wrapped in bright green and red. In moments, Aunt Della had him a grizzly-grip again, saying, "Just look at you. How big you done got. Why I remember when you was so little. Now you a young man, and a handsome one too." Jamal blushed.

"Boy's a 'rassler now, Della. Watch out. He might bear hug you back," said Pop.

"Let him try. He can't out-hug me."

"Jamal, help me get these bags into your room. You'll stay in the other room, the one I fixed up for you. Got your sleeping bag in there. Get some of your clothes and move them in there too. Won't be but a few days."

"Yes sir." Jamal picked up the three suitcases and headed to his small bedroom to put them on the bed. Aunt Della headed to the kitchen.

"Let's see what we got to work with in here," she said, as she entered. "I can already tell I got to go the grocery store. Lonny, you never did keep a real kitchen."

The remainder of the day was a busy one. Aunt Della took Jamal to the store with her, and the two older men did what older men did: tinkered in the garage, fooled with the old pickup, talked of the "good old days," which seemed to get better with each passing year. God, Jamal thought, I hope I don't get like that. *But I probably will.*

The grocery store was packed. Folks have twelve months' notice about the holidays, yet they wait until the last minute to get the stuff they need. Adults. With Aunt Della leading the charge, Jamal worked each aisle of the Piggly Wiggly, getting whatever his aunt instructed. By the time they got to the checkout, Jamal was steering a full two baskets of food. Who was going to eat all this food? Pop and he wouldn't have to cook for months; the leftovers would feed them until spring.

With Jamal steering the two baskets out the front door of the store, his Aunt Della stopped at the vendor in front of the store. Christmas trees. "Boy, we need a tree too. Your granddaddy is a Scrooge, no tree or wreath or nothing at that house. Let's pick us one out."

"What we gonna' decorate it with?" asked Jamal.

"We'll figure out something. Your grandmother, bless her soul, had a bunch of stuff for decorating. I bet it's still there. I'll find it. Pick us out a good one. We'll decorate it tonight after supper."

Jamal did as instructed, though he had no idea of what to look for in a Christmas tree. "Just get a full one," his aunt told him. What's a "full" tree look like? Jamal picked one he thought looked full. His aunt paid for it. "We got a deal on that. That's the trick. Get the tree on Christmas Eve, and it's cheaper. Don't nobody want to keep a bunch of trees they can't sell after December 24." Jamal loaded the tree into the trunk of his aunt's car, tying down the trunk and the two trekked home. It was mid-afternoon when they arrived. As Jamal helped his complaining grandfather – "Damn tree gonna' have needles all over my floor, Della. Then I go to clean it all up." – set up the tree, the house slowly filled with wonderful aromas: the workings of his aunt in the kitchen. She had brought some items, mostly deserts, with her from Mississippi. More people, church folks, arrived, maybe eight or ten – people Jamal had never seen in his life. They acted as if they knew him, but he was clueless as to who they were. They acted like they were long-lost uncles, aunts and cousins who hadn't seen him since he was a little baby. The older women kept coming by and squeezing his cheeks. Why do they do this? Is it some requirement that when women hit a certain age, they must pinch the cheeks of young folks? Though he didn't know these people, Jamal felt oddly, or maybe not, at ease, at home even. This was the "family-thing" he hoped for. It eased the void present by his mom's absence. He missed her greatly, but the scene at Pop's house on this day alleviated much of the angst.

At 6:00 PM, dinner was served. The table had been set earlier with all the nice plates and stuff. Pop and Jamal never ate on these plates. Jamal thought his Aunt Della had brought them with her, but it was all his late grandmother's. With the table set, the food was brought in. It resembled a parade, with everyone watching as Aunt Della directed where each item of the meal would be set on the table: a huge turkey, large pans of dressing, bowls of yams and greens, and a basket of rolls. It all smelled so good and looked even better. It was shame to tear into it, thought Jamal; it looked so nice. Famous chefs couldn't do any better.

The meal itself was delicious, but the conversations were even better. With Jamal the only kid present, the topics were out of his reach, but the tone, the jokes, and the laughter weren't. Pop was truly enjoying himself, as he and his "peers" replayed events and stories from the past. He smiled, he laughed, he actually talked – a lot – at the dinner table, something Jamal had never seen. There was reverent talk of his late grandmother,

Claire. Everyone loved her, especially Pop. Aunt Della, Claire's older sister, reminded everyone of her younger sister's smarts and athletic ability in high school. "Jamal, I bet you get that from her. She was a basketball player and track runner. That girl could run like the wind. And she could dance up a storm. All the boys liked her. Instead, she went with that one there." Aunt Della pointed toward Pop. It was a good-natured jest and reminded Jamal of the old TV show Sanford and Son, where Fred and Aunt Esther used to banter back and forth. He never heard "fish-eyed fool" from Aunt Della, but the evening was young yet. Pop and Della had that sort of relationship it seemed to Jamal, a sort of friendly dislike, if that was possible. Pop had come and taken Della's younger sister away, and Della had to remind him of it every chance she could. Of course, the two loved each other – always had – but it would go against form to act it.

"Jamal, eat up," ordered Jamal's "Aunt Mary," who was not his aunt, just another of the adopted temporary family. He called her "aunt," not feeling the least bit odd about it.

"I'm dieting a little," answered Jamal. "I can only eat certain things."

"Nonsense, boy, eat up. When you gonna' eat like this again. No growing boy needs to be on a diet. What you dieting for? You thin as a rail."

"I'm on the wrestling team at school."

"Wrestling team? You mean like I see on TV?"

"Not exactly," answered Jamal.

Lonny jumped in. "It's 'rasslin'" – Pop still had trouble saying the word properly – "like they do in the Olympics. It is like boxing in a way, you know, Golden Gloves and stuff. I seen him once. Boy is pretty good. Jamal, go get your medal from that tournament and show 'em. Coach says the kid is a natural."

Jamal felt a bit embarrassed by all the attention.

"Go on, get that medal. Show it to 'em."

What was this? Lonny proud of Jamal? Jamal went to his room, got his medal and showed it to everyone. Aunt Della gushed over it, like it was an Olympic medal. “Look at that. Little Jamal, a tough guy, a wrestler.” She was then back to his diet. “Well, that don’t mean you can’t eat one day a year. When you think you’ll eat like this again? You won’t, not with that one there.” She again pointed in the direction of Pop.

“Hush up Della, me and the boy eat just fine,” Pop fired back. “And we do it without a lot of hens cackling at the table.”

Aunt Della ignored Pop. “What stuff can you eat, Jamal? We got plenty here. Gotta’ be something you can eat.”

“Coach says green is good, that anything green, I can eat as much of as I want.”

She didn’t hesitate, grabbing his plate and putting an extra helping of greens on it. “Dig in,” she encouraged. “And save some room for some pie.”

Sweet potato pie. Yummmmmy, thought Jamal. Coach Russo would understand. If he ate two pieces, he figured he could run some extra each day to get rid of it until he was back in school and at practice.

After dinner, the mob moved to the living room and the naked tree that sat in front of the window. “I found the lights and stuff,” Aunt Della said. “They was out in the garage. *He”* – she pointed in the direction of Lonny – “ put them in a box in the back of the garage. Ain’t used them in years, the old Scrooge.”

“Shut that yap, Della,” retorted Lonny. “Woman never shuts up. Wilson, get this woman to close that mouth of hers. You her husband.”

“Don’t bring me into this. I gotta’ sleep with her,” deadpanned Uncle Wilson.

Jamal laughed to himself. This was turning out to be a great holiday.

The entire “family” adorned the tree with lights and all sorts of trimmings. Popcorn had even been popped and stringed to decorate the tree with. Jamal enjoyed it all. It was fun to see the adults all engaged and in a festive mood, especially Lonny.

With the tree decorated, everyone crammed into the small living room, using dining room chairs to seat those folks the living room's furniture wouldn't. The conversation varied – sports, work, young folks, the good old days. Jamal sat and took it all in. The men soon went into the kitchen. Time for Pop's "special" eggnog. Jamal didn't know what eggnog was, so needless to say, he had no idea of Pop's "special" eggnog. His grandfather came out of the kitchen and gave him some. "Sip on this, boy," he said.

Jamal took a big gulp, and nearly spit it out. When the milky concoction hit his throat, it was like a rocket being launched, complete with the whistling sound. When it hit his stomach, it exploded like some sort of bomb. Jamal nearly spit it out and coughed, causing his grandfather and the other men to laugh out loud. What's in that?" asked Jamal.

"Put hair on your chest, boy" answered Pop, which was no answer at all. "A little bourbon is all."

"I don't think I want anymore," said Jamal. "I'll stick to regular milk."

Lonny laughed again. The men continued to sit and talk in the kitchen, enjoying the "Pop specialty."

Near ten o'clock, Jamal said his good nights to everyone and went to bed. Despite the noise from the other room, sleep found Jamal quickly. He woke up at 1:00 AM, and the noise had dissipated a little. By 3:00 AM, all was quiet. The temporary kinfolk had left, leaving Aunt Della and Uncle Wilson, tucked away in Jamal's room. Jamal went back to sleep for the night.

The next morning, Jamal arose and had his day welcomed with more wonderful smells from the kitchen. He jumped up and started for the kitchen, when something caught his eye in the corner of the room: a computer and printer were on the small room's desk. What was this? As if planned, Lonny entered the room and asked, "What you got there boy? Santa must have snuck in here last night."

"Santa? Ain't seen him in years. He didn't come to the south side of Chicago much."

"Yeah, well he still comes to north Memphis."

"Whose is this?" asked Jamal.

"Boy, I imagine it's yours. I ain't got no use for a damn computer."

Jamal went to the terminal and looked on the monitor. A tag was there: To Jamal, From Santa. Jamal hadn't believed in Santa Claus in years. It came from his grandfather. When he looked at his grandfather, all he said, "Merry Christmas, Jamal. I hope you like it."

"I do." Jamal was stunned.

"People told me that the thing would do all the things any new one will do. Type stuff up, play games, and get on the Internets—"

"You mean 'Internet,'" Jamal interrupted.

"Yeah, Internet. It'll help you with school. It's working now. I got the cable TV people to come out and hook it all up earlier this week. Your uncles came in here last night and set it up. I got a basic cable TV package too. You can watch more on TV now. Go on in there and look."

Jamal ran into the other room. A new TV replaced the older box one. The tree they had put up the night before was now surrounded with presents. He looked closely. Many of them were for him, while a few were for his granddad. Aunt Della and Uncle Wilson were there. "Get over there and tear into them, boy," ordered his uncle. "I want to see what people got you."

Jamal did as instructed. He had eight boxes with his name on them. Four of them came from Pop. The other four simply had "From: The Family" on the tag. Jamal tore into them. There were clothes, video games,

games for the computer, an MP3 player, some new boots. Lonny came back into the room with another box. "This came yesterday from your Mom."

Jamal took the package and examined it. Unlike the other boxes, he opened this one gently. It was from his Mom, after all. There was a card inside. He opened it and read it to himself:

"Dear Jamal,

I hope this Christmas is a happy one for you. I only regret I am not there to be with you. I will be soon, but not in time for the holiday. I hope you and Pop are getting along well. I miss you so much. And though this is not enough to make up for the damage I have done, I hope you enjoy it and get some use from it. From what I hear from your grandfather, I think you will. It took me some time to find exactly what you needed. It took two trips to get it. We were allowed to shop once a week. The first week, I couldn't find what you needed. The second week, I did.

I am doing fine. I feel so much better. I have been told that if I progress like I have been, I could be out of here in January. We will see.

Until then, Merry Christmas, and remember how much I love you. I cannot wait to see you. I am counting the hours until I do.

Love always,

Momma

P.S.

I will call you soon, maybe Christmas day."

Jamal nearly began crying. He hadn't opened the box. "What's in the box, boy? That's the point of presents. Open it!" said Pop.

Jamal did as he was told. He was completely shocked by what he found: a brand new pair of blue Adidas wrestling shoes and matching wrestling headgear. There was also a pair of new gym shorts, a matching t-shirt and three pairs of athletic socks.

"Look at all that," said Pop. "Those shoes even match your school colors. They are sharp. Might need to get me some of those and get to working out again."

Jamal was speechless. His Christmas, which he had dreaded, had just turned out perfect. No, near perfect. His Mother was stuck in some Chicago treatment place. If she were here, it would be perfect.

A huge breakfast awaited the four of them: eggs prepared to order, pancakes, sausage, bacon, and biscuits. A perfect ending to a perfect twenty-four period.

"Merry Christmas, Jamal," said his grandfather, as they headed to the table. "I'm good to have you here."

— Thirteen —

One of the first things Jamal did with his new computer was go to the Chicago Tribune website. Though the computer wasn't new – it had been used by Pop's church – it was a good one, one that surfed the web fast. The Tribune page pulled up instantly. Jamal wanted to see what was going on in his old stomping ground. A familiar face popped up on the websites first page: Travis Holloway. Jamal read further; the article's headline told him all he needed to know: "Holiday violence claims life of South Side teen." Jamal read the first paragraph: "A shooting on the city's south side left one teen dead and two in the hospital. Travis Holloway, 16, was killed following an earlier altercation with another teen. Samuel French and Patrick Rice, both 15, were also shot and are in critical condition at The University of Chicago Medical Center. A 'person of interest' is being sought in the case. Reasons for the shooting and the argument that prompted it are not clear at the present time. Funeral arrangements for Holloway have not yet been made." The article continued with comments from neighbors. Most spoke of the dangerous area that had once been a nice place. Other comments were about the "out of control" teenagers and the gangs that welcomed them into their ranks. Jamal simply stared at the image looking back at him; it was the school photo Travis took just that school year. Jamal remembered how Samuel, Patrick and himself made fun of the "goofy" look in the picture. One of the three cracked that it looked like a "mug shot."

Both a sense of sadness and relief swept over Jamal. Sadness because of his friend's death; relief because of his own safety. Jamal knew that had he been in Chicago, he'd have been with the three. He might be in the hospital with Samuel and Patrick, near death, or he might have been killed like Travis. He didn't know whether to cry or jump for joy.

Suddenly, Jamal heard a voice over his shoulder. It was his grandfather. "What you reading, boy?

Jamal didn't answer right away. "It's an article in the Chicago paper," he finally answered. "It's about one of my friends."

"What's it about? Something good, I hope."

"It isn't. Look for yourself," said Jamal, giving his seat to his grandfather.

"Let me see it," Pop sat and read the first few lines of the article. "How does this internet, computer stuff work?"

"You have to scroll down," Jamal told him,

"Scroll down? What the hell does that mean?"

"Use the mouse, Pop."

"I don't see no mouse."

"Not a real mouse. The thing by your right hand. That's a mouse." Jamal took control over his grandfather's shoulder, scrolling the article down to where his grandfather could read it. Lonny read for a minute or so.

"I see. Can't say I'm surprised by it. You shouldn't be either."

Jamal stayed silent, still stunned by the news.

"I hate to say it, Jamal, but you'd have been right there with them. That could have been you. Still could be if you don't turn things completely around, like you been trying to do. Thank God, you got sent to me. I'd hate to have to see you in a box, like that Travis boy's folks are gonna' have to do. It's real sad. I know you are bothered, but say a little prayer that it wasn't you." Pop let his words sink in. "What it say about the other two boys? They okay?"

"The article says they in the hospital, in critical condition."

"That's sad. Three families ruined – four, if you count the boy that's done it and gonna' get sent to prison. Just sad."

"Pop, you think Samuel and Patrick are gonna' make it?"

"I don't know. Gunshot wounds can be real nasty injuries. Mess up your insides something fierce. Maybe we can call the hospital later today and see how they are doing. That is, if the hospital will tell us anything. We ain't the boys' family, you know. They got privacy rights and stuff at hospitals."

"I hope we can. What time do you think we can call? I'd really like to know how they are doing. They're my best friends in the world."

"Later this afternoon, we'll try. I sure hope they are okay. We don't need any more young black boys shot dead in the street over nonsense. Maybe this shooting will wake the two of 'em up." Pop then got up from the desk and headed toward the small room's door. "Jamal, why don't you come out back and help me in the garage. I got some things to move around that I can't get by myself. We'll come back in and try to call later after lunch."

Jamal said, "Sure. I'll be right there. Let me shut the computer down."

That computer image of Travis stayed with Jamal the entire day. He helped his grandfather in the garage, the image of his dead friend not far from his mind. After the work in the garage, he got on his sweat suit and took a two-mile run around the block. The Christmas meal had to be worked off. The team would practice one more time when the varsity got back from Chattanooga.

It wasn't a two-mile block, but he had calculated that six times around it was two miles. After his run, he went into the house and found his grandfather on the phone. Pop signaled to Jamal that this was the hospital on the phone.

"Yes ma'am. I understand. Thanks for your help." Pop hung up the phone and looked at Jamal. The look said it all.

"What is it, Pop?" Lonny's face told him everything he needed to know. "They didn't make it, did they?"

"I'm afraid not, Jamal. I am so sorry."

Jamal stood in stunned silence. Just like that – the snap of your fingers – he'd lost three friends. Dead, as in never to return. Teenagers just like him. He couldn't speak. When he did, all he could say was, "Pop, I think I'm gonna' go to my room for a while."

"You do that. Son, I am so sorry. I know they was your friends, your best friends. God, I wish this hadn't have happened."

Around dinnertime – "supper-time" in his grandfather's southern home – Pop yelled to Jamal to come to the phone. Jamal got up from his bed – he hadn't slept, just thought – and went into the living room where Pop's phone was located. "Hello," Jamal said into the phone.

"Baby-boy, how are you?" It was Anna. Jamal immediately forgot the awful news that greeted his day.

"Mom! How come you didn't call yesterday, on Christmas?"

"I didn't want to call. Well, I did, but I didn't want to spend the whole time on the phone crying and all. I was so sad yesterday knowing that my child had to spend the day without me. So I said I'll just call tomorrow when I am in better shape. I'm sorry, but I didn't want to bawl like a baby. Did you get the shoes?"

"Yes. They are great. Fit like a glove. And they match our uniforms too. So does the headgear."

"I had a tough time getting that stuff. I didn't know what wrestling shoes or a headgear even looked like. A man here at the hospital used to wrestle, and he helped me pick it all out. We get one shopping trip a week. The first week I didn't have a clue. The second week, this man helped me. I am so glad it all fit and was the right color. Your grandfather gave me the info on the colors and all. He was the one who told me what to get you. I had no idea of what you might want or need. He said you was using some old shoes the coach give you. Said shoes might be a good thing to buy, as well as a headgear. So I bought it three days before the holiday. I didn't know if they'd get to you. Your grandfather paid for me to FedEx it to you."

"They're perfect. I tried them on the minute I opened them. I'll try them out when we go back to practice. How are you feeling? You gonna' get out soon?"

"Could be real soon. And I am feeling great. I haven't felt this good in years, since I…I…well, you know."

"I know. I can't wait for you to get out and for me to move back to Chicago."

"That might not happen. I might be coming there and staying there for a while. The doctors seem to think it would be best to start over in a new place, away from the crowd and surroundings that got me into trouble. But we'll see. Things aren't certain yet. I first have to keep making progress here. It shouldn't be too much longer. I'm doing really well. I've been doing a ton of reading. I need to get back in school and finish my degree. I have used the computer here, when I could, to research some things. Finishing school at night would be hard, but I could do it. We'll see. I got some great plans for us, and I can't wait to get started on them."

"I got a computer for Christmas. Maybe I can email you now."

"Your grandfather told me you got one. Said his church helped him get it. Said some people at the church and your Aunt Della and Uncle Wilson were there for the holiday."

"They were. It was great to see Aunt Della again. She's just like I remember her. And that sweet potato pie!"

"Yeah, it's good. Wish I had some. How'd she and your grandfather get along? There used to be some tension between them."

"It still is, but I think they like each other better. They just won't admit it."

"I think you're right. Always been that way with them. Since I was a little girl."

A moment of silence.

"Jamal, I read the paper today. I know what happened to your friends. I am so sorry."

"Yeah, I can't believe it. I been thinking about it all day. It just don't seem real to me. I was just with them not too long ago, and now they're gone."

"You be thankful. Well, not thankful that they're gone, but glad you wasn't up here, 'cause you'd have been with them, and I might not be talking to you now."

"Pop said the same thing."

"I know he did. He is so glad you are with him."

"He told me."

"And he means it. He loves you like you was his own. And you are in a way. You are my boy, and I am a part of him, which means you are too. Your grandfather loves you very much. He is tough. Was when I was a kid. But he always had my mom to smooth out his rough edges. He ain't been the same since Mom was killed. I see more of the old him since you been there though. Every time I have spoken with him, he's a little more like his old self. You been good for him."

"The man's hard and tough. I didn't think he even liked me for the first month I was here. It ain't been like it used to be, but it is getting better. He's still hard as a rock though. I think he'll be glad when you get well, and I am back with you."

"Don't say that. It ain't true. He just doesn't know how to express himself like that. He's old school, the strong, silent type. Like John Wayne."

"Who?"

"John Wayne, an old actor. Tough guy. It doesn't matter. What does matter is that he loves you much. And don't forget it. If he is hard, it is for your own good. I hear it's working. Your grades are good. You're doing great in wrestling. You're helping him out around the house. You're going to church. Things are good, I hear."

"Yeah, I guess. I don't have time to get into any trouble. Coach keeps me busy with wrestling every day after school and on Saturdays. At night, I am studying and doing homework. Grades have to be good to stay on the team. On Sundays, I am at church. I don't have time for anything else."

"Pop tells me your grades are good. Says you are a real good wrestler too. He said he saw you once, and you did really well. He also told me you won a medal at a tournament."

"Yeah, second place. I'm gonna' get first place next time at the City Championships at the end of January."

"I bet you will. I hope I get to see you. If you get some pictures, save me some."

"I can send them with an email."

"I guess that'll work. I get computer time each week. I don't think pictures are a problem. These people monitor our Internet activity. Some stuff is off-limits."

"I'll send some if I get any."

"I have to get off the phone, but I will call again real soon. Are you okay? With your friends, I mean."

"I don't know how I feel. I am sad, but I am also glad I wasn't there. It don't make no sense to me though. Travis, Samuel and Patrick, they were just like me. And now they're gone."

"I know. It's horrible. I am so sorry for you. I knew those boys too. Sort of. They just got mixed up with the wrong things. Now, they're gone because of it. I hope you see a lesson in all of this. Through all your sadness, find the lesson. It's there, and it's clear."

"I know. I don't want to end up like them. I don't, but I am so sad it happened to them. I didn't even get to say goodbye."

"That's life. It's a fragile thing. This also teaches you to cherish each day, to cherish your friends because you never know when it will all end. Tomorrow is promised to no one."

"I see."

"I have to get off this phone. You be good. I love you, and so does your grandfather. Hopefully, the next time I speak to you, I will be telling you when I get out of here."

"Me too."

"Jamal, I love you, and you take care of yourself and your grandfather."

"I love you too. I will, though Pop doesn't need anyone to take care of him. He does just fine by himself."

Anna laughed. "You are right. I will talk with you soon."

"Bye. I love you, Mom."

Jamal hung up the phone. Lonny was standing there. Jamal was so into the conversation; he didn't know he was around.

"She doing okay, boy?" he asked.

"Said she is doing fine. Might get released soon."

"Well, I hope so. I hope she never has to go through such mess again."

"Me too."

"How are you? It's got to be tough to lose some friends like you did."

"It's weird. I am sad, but at the same time, I am so glad I wasn't with them. I almost feel guilty 'cause I feel this way."

"Don't. Them boys got into some stuff they shouldn't have. Don't feel guilty because you weren't there. You might not be here if you were. Be glad."

"I am. I just can't believe I am never gonna' see them again."

"That is tough. Death is forever. Learn it. Remember it. Life is a fragile thing. Don't take anything for granted. Tomorrow is promised for no one."

"That's what Mom just told me."

"It's true. You got to live right. Live life to the fullest. You got a second chance when you got sent here. Take advantage of it."

"I will try to." Pause. "What we eating tonight?"

"Leftover Christmas dinner. Your Aunt Della left us enough to eat for a week. Woman talks too much, but she sure can cook."

"That's true."

"Let's get in there and get after it, boy. When we finish, you can show me how to operate this cable stuff we got. That remote control looks like something you'd run a spaceship with."

Jamal laughed. "Yes sir."

— Fourteen —

January was the busiest and most important part of the entire wrestling season. The varsity wrestlers were competing for seeding at the Region 8 tournament, while the freshmen wrestlers were vying with their freshmen opponents for seeding at the city tournament. With two and sometimes three matches during the week and tournaments on each weekend, the schedule was crowded. Practice was on the non-match days. There literally was no time off in January.

The month had been a good one for Jamal. Going into the final week of January, he had amassed a 15-2 record, his only losses for the season coming to his North High adversary Colin Young. Coach Russo told Jamal that if things play out, as they appeared they would, he would be the number two seed in the city tourney. "That's good. It usually means a first round bye and an easier road to the medal round. I think you can get in the finals, and you'll get another shot at the North kid. You been looking good this month. You haven't lost, and you've been dominant. Each week, it seems you get better and better."

The tournament was one week away. It was oddly being held on a Thursday, an unusual occurrence, since tournaments were often too long to be held on school nights. This tournament was a double elimination event, but each school was only allowed one person per weight class, as opposed to "open" events where each school could place as many as they wanted in each of the fourteen weight-classes. Kennedy did well each year at the Freshman City Championships, as witnessed by the small banners in the gym, as well as the varsity lineup, which was filled with former Freshman City Champions. The team finished second last year. Even with just twelve wrestlers – two spots short of a full lineup – Coach Russo felt this year's lineup was capable of winning the tournament. He was pressing the freshmen hard on practice days, while reminding them of their opponents coming up in the city tourney: "Jamal, Colin ain't practicing like you are; he's working hard to win the city." Little jabs designed to motivate and, frankly, piss off the individual wrestlers. And he got onto everyone. The man memorized every match of every wrestler he coached; he remembered them and would remind wrestlers of losses or mistakes – anything to turn the screws and challenge each kid. Some kids didn't respond well to his tactics, but it mattered little; Coach Russo wanted everyone to be mentally, as well as physically tough.

• •

The next Wednesday, Sycamore High School brought their freshmen team to Kennedy for a match. It wasn't an "official" match, but more a scrimmage. It would be played out like a real match, with a real referee and all. The gym was set up just as it would be for a real match. The only difference was it was the freshman only. They were the headliners, instead of the varsity. Coach Russo saw it as opportunity for the freshmen team to "strut its stuff," but also as a warm-up for the city tournament, which would follow the next night. The event was also a fund-raiser of sorts for the wrestling team. The entire freshmen team had sold tickets to their classmates and teachers. All the concessions from the night would go to the wrestling team. It was an event Coach Russo started several years earlier, and it turned out to be a good thing. The freshmen team took it very seriously; they didn't want to look bad in front of their classmates. They also didn't want to embarrass the tough program Kennedy had become. With the varsity team members running the scorer's table and the concession stand, the freshmen team wanted to prove themselves to their older teammates.

The gym was nearly full. It was a bigger crowd than Coach Russo had expected. It seemed the entire freshmen class was present and seated somewhere in the gym. Music filled the air, as the huge blue mat sat idle in the middle of the gym. Sycamore would come out first and warm-up. Sycamore High School was a Memphis Public School located in the southeast part of the city. It once was a county school that became a city school some years back. The school, because it was located out east, was thought to be wealthy like the suburban and private schools located in the area. It wasn't. The student body at Sycamore was only slightly more advantaged than the Kennedy kids. Perception, however, was the reality; the Sycamore kids were "just another of the rich kids from out east" to most Kennedy wrestlers and students.

The Sycamore team ran out to the mat amid many boos coming from the Kennedy fans. Most of the students in the stands didn't understand the sport of wrestling and its inherent "good sportsmanship." Jamal had learned this as the season progressed. There was little booing at wrestling meets; polite applause or pleasant indifference typically accompanied a meet. However, the fans cheered heartily for the home team.

The team's captains met at the mat's center and shook hands. Jamal got chosen a captain for the match. He didn't know what that would entail, but he still felt proud of it. The referee, after flipping his red/green disc, looked to Jamal and asked, "Even or odd?" Jamal didn't know what to answer or why, but he said, "Odd." This meant the weight class that would get the choice at the first period breaks in a match.

Tonight's match would start with the 171-pound weight class. Mark Little, the Kennedy wrestler, was the freshmen team's "weak" link. He had won about as many matches he lost, his record for the season hovering near .500. Tonight would be one of Mark's "good nights." The referee blew his whistle and began the match. Mark rushed right at his opponent and snatched him up in a head and arm throw – a headlock and hip toss. His opponent went right to his back, and the referee began his count. Several seconds later, he hit the mat, signaling a pin. The Kennedy crowd roared its approval. Wrestling was like a fight, and there was nothing some of the students loved more than a good scrap.

Jamal would go next to last tonight. He weighed in at 152 pounds even. He could have weighed more, as every team was given a two-pound allowance beginning in late December. He had learned to control his dieting, so he didn't need the allowance. Even with his holiday feasting, he still came back to practice in January just one and a half pound over his weight, which was much better than some of his teammates, even the varsity guys. Some of them came in seven and eight pounds over. One varsity wrestler, Kenny Long, came in a full ten pounds over his weight-class. Hurts to be him, thought Jamal. Gonna' take a bunch of work to get that off in such a short time. A lot of moving and little eating.

It was to be a good night for Kennedy. Of the twelve matches wrestled, the team lost just one – Jamal's. The Sycamore wrestler was not all that strong or even that technical, but he "caught" Jamal with a lateral drop and pinned him in the first period. The referee blew his whistle, and Jamal rushed his opponent. The crowd, his classmates, had him all hyped up, doing little thinking. He was completely out of his game, playing to the crowd. He tied up with his opponent, pushing him backward. Pushing is not the right word; it was more like trying to run through his opponent. When Jamal did this, his opponent simply applied – tightly – an overhook to one arm and an underhook to the other and went straight back to his back, turning his body at the last second and putting the rushing Jamal right onto his back. The Sycamore kid used Jamal's own momentum to his advantage. Jamal squirmed and fought to get to his belly to no avail. The Sycamore wrestler had him stuck. If it had been late in the period, Jamal might have been able to hold out, but he could not hold on for an entire two-minute period. The referee slapped the mat right beside Jamal's head. He could hear it better than anyone. He got off the mat, went to the center circle, saw the referee raise his opponent's hand and then he went to the opposing coach to shake his hand before going back to the Kennedy bench. There was that feeling again – all eyes were on him, the "loser."

Coach Russo told him to sit by him. When Jamal took his seat, Coach Russo watched the start of the last match. He then spoke to Jamal as he monitored the action on the mat. "Let that be a lesson to you. Don't play to the crowd. They don't know what the heck is going on or what you are trying to do. They just want to see a fight. You can beat that kid nine out of ten times. That was his one win. You might see him again tomorrow night. Get you a sip, and get on the bench."

Sycamore was no match for Kennedy. The final score was 65-18, Kennedy. The only weak link tonight was Jamal and his careless effort. Coach Russo was right; that was not Jamal at his best. He hoped he would get another shot at the kid at the City Championships tomorrow. He was still the number two seed. Coach Russo had told him before he left the school that night that the match was not official, so the kid's win would not affect the tournament's seeding. Though that was a relief, tomorrow would not be a good day at school. He knew he was going to hear it from his classmates who were there to see it. He braced up for it, knowing he would start hearing it first thing in homeroom. Just ignore it, he thought. Besides, none of them were out on the team, so it didn't mean anything. Just words.

When he got home that night, Pop was finishing up a phone call. He hung the phone up and said, "Good news, boy. Your momma is on her way home. I just got her a ticket on the bus. She is leaving at midnight tonight, maybe later because of the snow up there. I told her I'd get her a plane ticket for tomorrow, but she said no, that she wanted to head south now and not tomorrow. Any event, she'll be here tomorrow."

"Are you sure?"

"Yes sir. She said January. Well, it is late-January, almost February. I'm gonna' pick her up when she gets in."

"That is great. I can't wait to see her."

"I know. I thought you'd take a day off tomorrow and be here when she gets here. I know she want to see you. The three of us might go get some lunch or something, or maybe –"

Jamal cut him off. "I can't miss school tomorrow. The City Championships are tomorrow night. I have to be at school to be in it."

"Yeah, but I thought you'd want to be here when she got in."

"I do, Pop, but I got to go the city. It's what I have been working on all year. Coach says I can win it."

"Yeah, but it's your momma. She sure gonna' want to see you."

"Bring her to the tournament. I can see her there. You can both watch the tournament. Maybe I can take the next day off."

"Boy, this ain't like you. Here I am, giving you a chance to miss school, and you want to go. Don't make sense. Can't say I am disappointed though. Two months ago, you couldn't stand school, and now you want to go. I guess that's a good thing."

"It's the tournament. I want to win that thing. I want to get that boy that beat me, that Colin kid."

"How'd you do tonight?"

"I lost. Made a dumb mistake and got pinned. But it don't matter. I'm gonna' make up for it tomorrow. Promise me, you'll bring Mom."

"Okay. What time and where?"

"We will go right after school. It is supposed to start at 4:00 PM at Germantown High School." It was a big high school just east of Memphis in Germantown, an affluent suburb of Memphis.

Pop said, "Is this the Germantown city championships? Why would the Memphis city tournament be in Germantown?"

"I don't know. Maybe they got a big gym or something."

"We'll try to get there boy. I don't know what time exactly she's getting' in, but if she is here in time, we'll be there."

"I'll call from school tomorrow at lunch to see if she is here. I'm tired. I think I'm gonna' hit the rack, Pop."

"Yeah, big day tomorrow. If you want something to eat, there's food in the refrigerator. Good night, Jamal."

"Night Pop."

— Fifteen —

Nerves. All day long, the nerves were ever present, like some cloud hanging over his head. Jamal had trouble concentrating in class. His mind only on one thing: the City Championships that night. Even his mother's arrival could not push the tournament off his front page. He did feel a little guilty about that, but he rationalized it, saying his Mom would understand setting and achieving goals. This was important. Freshman city champions often went onto become state champions; look at Derrick Slater. He'd won the freshman city title three years earlier, and last year, he stood atop the medal stand at the state tournament in Nashville. Of course, Jamal didn't know what his future in wrestling was beyond this year, but he was living in the present; he'd deal with the future when it got here.

Coach Russo had announced that the freshmen wrestlers would be going to the city championships during the morning announcements. Many a well-wisher said, "Good luck" to Jamal and the other frosh wrestlers in the halls that day. The team was set to leave after lunch, as the weigh-in was at 1:00 PM. It would take almost an hour to get to Germantown High School and be there on *Coach Russo's time* – fifteen minutes early. Coach Russo instructed the team to meet in the practice gym after A lunch, the first lunch period at Kennedy. They would check weight and get on the road.

At lunch, the wrestlers sat together in the cafeteria. Coach Russo made a run through the cafeteria, checking to see what the guys were eating. He already had a working agreement with the cafeteria manager and staff to monitor the wrestler's eating. In fact, a certain section on the line was food specifically for wrestlers only: salads, fruit, and little else. The list of food that the wrestlers *couldn't eat* – pizza, cookies, hamburgers, bread, French fries (all the good stuff) – was much longer than the stuff they could nibble on, "nibble" being the operative word. Of course, the wrestlers had friends, and they used their friends to get forbidden food. It was like a black market one used to find in communist countries, except the commodities were Snickers bars and Skittles instead of Levis. His trip to the wrestlers' training table today yielded one chicken sandwich, a bag of butter cookies, and an order of French fries. He gave all of it to the students at the table next to the wrestlers. "You can eat this in March," he said, as he snatched up the, what he called, "contraband." "You got to make weight in about two hours. Win the city title and gorge yourself tonight."

It was Noon when the wrestling team left Kennedy. Everyone's weight was right on target. Jamal weighed 150.2 pounds. Two pounds to spare. Everything is going according to plan, thought Jamal.

The freshmen traveled to Germantown in a new blue van today. Having to leave before 3:00 PM meant the team couldn't get a bus, so Coach Russo rented a van. It was a fifteen passenger van. It was a bit tight. Coach had done this before. He told the guys over 160 pounds to get on the back two seats, with everyone else in the front two seats of the van. "Squeeze in. You'll fit. Gonna' have to. This is all we got." Jamal was crammed into the second seat with four other smaller guys. With all the gym bags and team gear, there wasn't an inch of the van that wasn't occupied.

The team arrived at Germantown and weighed in. The schools were being weighed in alphabetically, so the crew from Kennedy was somewhere in the middle of the pack. The brackets had already been done and were posted on a wall in the lobby of the gymnasium. With every school in the area with a freshmen team in attendance, the brackets were full. The 152-pound weight class had a sixteen man bracket. Jamal looked to find his name. It was in the middle of the bracket. Coach Russo came up behind him. "Somehow you got seeded third. That is what it means when you are on that line in the bracket. This guy is second." He pointed to the name on the bottom line of the bracket. He then moved his hand to the top. "Your friend is seeded number one." Colin Young of North High School. "That's who we want in the finals. Win four in a row, and you're a city champion."

"I thought I would be number two," Jamal said, even though it was more like a question.

"I did too. Didn't work out that way. Coaching politics. I argued for you to be, but I finally said number three would be okay, that we'd beat the kid in the semi-finals. Sometimes these seeding meetings turn into a pissing match for the coaches. Don't sweat it, you'll do fine."

The Kennedy team jogged around the entire gym and then took a place on one the mats to warm-up. It was after two o'clock now. School would be letting out soon. Jamal wondered if Pop had picked up his mom yet, or if she was even in town yet. Pop said they *might* make it. While Jamal hoped they could make it, another side of him sort of didn't want his Mom in the stands. If nerves got him when she wasn't there, what would they do to him if she was? He'd hate to get all nervous and tight on today. Worse, he would hate to have his Mom see him get beat.

Wrestling tournaments don't usually start on time; at least, not the one Jamal had been a part of. If the ticket said things would start at 9:00 AM, you could count on it actually beginning at 9:30, at the earliest. People don't make weight or don't show up. When that happens, an entire bracket has to be reseeded and redrawn, which means the seeding debate begins anew with the coaches. Or as Coach Russo would say, "The pissing match is started over." Today's event was set to start at 2:00. Three o'clock was more likely the time things would get going.

Jamal went to look at the bracket again. His early visit was to see where he was seeded. He didn't even see who his opponent would be. He was surprised: Nick Sully of Sycamore High, the very kid who had pinned him last night. *That won't happen today, thought Jamal.* Coach Russo was right again: you never know when you'll get another shot at someone who beat you. Even though last night's match was a glorified exhibition, it was still a loss in Jamal's mind; he would try to even up the score today.

Four huge and colorful mats covered the entire gym floor. A tote board with all sixteen schools in attendance was on one of the gym's walls. The schools were listed in alphabetical order. Jamal assumed each team's total team points would be placed on this board. The mats were covered with wrestlers, each team staking its own little corner of a mat. The Kennedy crew was on the black Rosewood High mat that sat next to the red Germantown mat. A St. Paul mat was present, as was a mat from White Station High School. All the schools were located close to Germantown. It all made sense to Jamal; why load-up and take a mat a long distance?

At 2:55 PM, the announcer told all the wrestlers to clear the mats. Things were getting ready to start. Jamal missed the start time by five minutes. As usual, the announcer told everyone to stay away from the mats unless they were "on deck" or "in the hole." This would keep traffic moving smoothly in the cramped gym. Coach Russo told the team that the order might go bit differently today due to some weight classes having more wrestlers in them than others. The 152-pound class was full, so it would be one of the first to be announced. He was correct: "Jamal Hayes of Kennedy High School and Nick Sully of Sycamore High, report to mat three."

Jamal made his way over to mat three, Coach Russo at his side. He and Sully were the third matchup called. They would be one of the first matches of the city tournament. With all four pairs of wrestlers set to go on the four mats, the announcer asked everyone to stand for the National Anthem. Odd, thought Jamal that this was not done earlier. It didn't help his nerves any to be standing two feet from his opponent, at attention looking to the gym's ceiling and the flag. When the anthem was done, the announcer did his best to imitate the boxing announcer Michael Buffer: "Let's get ready to rrrrrrrumble!!!!!!!" A horrible imitation. If imitation is the highest form of flattery, what was a bad imitation? Insulting flattery? That was like cussing someone out, but then saying, "You meant it in the best possible way."

Jamal and Sully had already checked in with the head table and were ready to go. The referee told them to shake 'em up, which the two did. On the blow of the whistle, Jamal wasted no time. Low single takedown. It had become his favorite takedown, one he could always count on. It worked. Four seconds into the match, and Jamal was up 2-0. That was as close as his Sycamore opponent would get. Hyped up for the match, Jamal was unstoppable this match. It was as if he'd been wrestling since birth; everything worked: low-single, chop and tilt, double, spiral, power-half, and the tight waist tilt. Every move he tried was successful. Jamal seemed to be one step ahead of his opponent at every turn. *Coach Russo was right; "One day, things will slow down, and you'll see everything."* The final score was 20-5, a technical fall, which happens when you get to a fifteen-point lead over your opponent. Jamal wanted to pin his Sycamore for, but Coach Russo told him a technical fall was sometimes better than a pin because it showed "complete domination."

The rest of the team did as well as Jamal did. The Freshman City Championships were off to a roaring start for the Kennedy Yellow jackets. All twelve Kennedy wrestlers won their first round matches, giving the team 46.5 points and the early lead in the event. Jamal looked at the tote board and was proud to see "Kennedy" atop the leader board.

The second round of the tournament would prove to be just as fruitful for the Kennedy crew, and Jamal would be one of the leaders. His opponent in the second round was a wrestler from Graceland High School in the Whitehaven part of the city. The school was named Graceland because it was near Graceland Mansion, the former home of Elvis Presley, the singer from a long time ago. Memphis had a lot of Elvis stuff in it. The school's nickname was the "Bulldogs." Jamal was surprised it wasn't the "Hound Dogs," being so close to the man's house.

His Graceland Bulldog opponent was no match; Jamal pinned him in the first period. After a quick double-leg takedown, Jamal grabbed his far arm and near ankle and put him right on his back. No trouble keeping him down. The match lasted all of :26 seconds.

Focused as he was on the tournament, Jamal couldn't help looking into the stands. Where were his grandfather and mother? Was her bus delayed? Did she even get to leave Chicago?

The second round of the tournament saw little change in the standings. Kennedy High School was still in the lead. Not a single Kennedy wrestler had lost a match yet. Even though the team was good, there were several wrestlers on the freshman team who had struggled at times this year, some losing as many as half their matches. Such was not the case thus far in the City Tournament. The Kennedy Yellow Jackets were on a roll.

The semi-finals were the next obstacle for Jamal. His opponent was someone he had wrestled early in January. He was a tough kid from Lutheran High School. Though Jamal had beaten him, he had just barely managed to do so, winning the match 6-5. Jamal got an escape with three seconds left in the match to get the win. In fact, with just a minute left in the bout, Jamal led 4-2, but gave up a takedown with ten seconds left in the match. Had he not stood up and escaped, the match would have gone into overtime, which would have seen both wrestlers go at for a minute, with the first person to get a takedown being the winner; Jamal didn't know if he had any gas left in his tank to go to overtime. He gave it all he had to get the escape and avoid overtime. He had no doubt this match would be just as tough.

Jamal wore the green ankle band. His foe, wearing a red and blue singlet, got the red ankle band. The referee had the wrestlers shake hands, blew the whistle, and it was on. Jamal immediately went for his new favorite takedown – the low single. No good. The kid was ready for it, and down-blocked the attempt, leaving Jamal in an awkward spot, prone and off –balance. The Lutheran wrestler saw his opportunity and took it, his cat-like reflexes allowing him to nearly hurdle Jamal's flat body to get behind him for control and the points. "Two takedown," said the referee. Jamal jumped to his feet and fought the hands that held him at his waist. Strong grip. He pushed down and pulled at his opponent's fingers. The Lutheran wrestler immediately lifted Jamal into the air and took him back down to the mat, causing a loud "thump" that caused a loud "whoa" from the crowd. It looked worse than it was, for Jamal was not injured in the least. A little out of air, but nothing major. He built up to his base and hit a sit-out, reaching up for his opponent's head. Sometimes wrestlers in the controlling position ride their opponent a little too high, allowing their head to be hooked and used to roll them onto their backs. Positions are reversed, as is control. The head roll wasn't there. Jamal kept moving, sitting out and turning, hoping to cause his opponent to get off balance and creating an angle for Jamal to reverse his opponent or escape. Nothing doing. Whenever Jamal sat out and turned, his opponent answered every move, not allowing the movement to upset his balance.

The wrestlers hit the outer circle of the mat, causing the referee to blow his whistle, ending the action and sending the two back to the center circle. Coach Russo twirled his finger in the air, making a circular action. It was his symbol for "buckeye," which meant "ditto," as in "same thing" – in other words, keep doing what you are doing. With a fresh start in the action, Jamal would try a different tactic to score. He had stood when his opponent got the first takedown and then worked for a reversal using mat moves. He would now stand again, hoping his opponent would be thinking Jamal would stay on the mat. It worked. The referee blew his whistle, and Jamal immediately stood and tore free. "One point, escape," said the referee.

The two combatants circled each other. Trimoli – his Lutheran high opponent's name was Stan Trimoli – body faked at Jamal as he circled to Jamal's right. Jamal did likewise, circling left. The time was running out on the first period; the clock at the corner of the mat was down to :21 seconds. *Take your time, thought Jamal. Set something up. No mistakes.* Trimoli tied Jamal up with a collar and elbow tie, pulling his head down and circling. He had Jamal's right wrist with his left hand, as he moved Jamal to the right. With a lightening-quick drop, Trimoli snapped Jamal's head down, letting his wrist go and dropping down to grab Jamal's ankle – ankle pick. Jamal was on his back for just a two count, but it was long enough for the referee to give back points to Trimoli. As the period ended, Jamal was down 6-2.

Jamal won the choice. Coach Russo signaled to him to take the down position. Jamal assumed the down position and readied himself. His mind raced: *stand-up, sit-out/turn-in, switch, head roll, or side roll.* Down by four going into the second period was no time to panic, but against a good opponent like Trimoli, making up a four point deficit would be tough. The referee asked Jamal if he was set; Jamal shook his head that he was. The Lutheran wrestler took his spot atop Jamal, and the whistle blew. Jamal was one step – no two steps – ahead of Trimoli. He stood up and tore free, his opponent having no time to counter it at all. When Trimoli rose to his feet, Jamal immediately took a shot at his legs, hoping once again to catch him off guard. It didn't work. Trimoli sprawled and kept Jamal at bay, pushing the top of his head down toward the mat. Jamal struggled to his feet, the weight of his opponent at the top of his shoulders. He backed out and moved more, faking at Trimoli with his arms, acting as if he were setting up another leg attack. Trimoli did the same. With the score 6-3, each wrestler knew the match's end was still very much in doubt. Both were cautious and leery of the other. Though Jamal had been taught numerous takedowns in his six weeks as a wrestler, he had only mastered a few. Each entered his mind: *low-single, double, head-reach single, front headlock. Got to set something up, he thought. Don't press. Let it happen.* The two continued to circle each other, reaching half-heartedly at each other, both trying to set up a takedown. The referee told both to get to work. It prompted a clash of heads. Both heard the referee and thought the same thing: be aggressive. Pummeling followed the clash of heads, each wrestler trying to get the advantage on their opponent. Jamal had tried everything he knew to no avail. Trimoli answered each set-up he tried. The period ended with the score 6-3, advantage Trimoli. In the break between periods, Coach Russo pulled Jamal in close and said, "He's gonna' try to stall it out. He will probably take down and either lie there or try to escape or reverse you and ride out the time to get the win. We got to make something happen. And now. Keep it simple. Keep him front of you and get after it."

Surprisingly, Trimoli chose neutral. Well, maybe not surprisingly. Jamal hadn't come close to getting a takedown today. Why not take neutral with an opponent who had no chance of taking you down? The two took their marks, and the referee blew the whistle, starting the third period of the semi-final match at 152 pounds. *Keep it simple."* Coach Russo's words stayed with him. He had tried everything he knew so far. Time to go back through his limited repertoire. With a small arm fake at his opponent, Jamal immediately dropped. *Low single.* It worked. Trimoli was caught by surprise; he teetered awkwardly, Jamal holding onto his right ankle. As Jamal leaned into Trimoli, he took control of his entire lower left leg and leaned even harder. Like the lumberjacks say, "Timber!" Trimoli fell to his side, Jamal working his way up and controlling Trimoli on the mat. The referee signaled the takedown. The score was now 6-5. Jamal looked for a wrist to ride. Placing his hands through Trimoli's armpits, he had both hands on his right wrist, but couldn't hold them. Trimoli got to his base quickly. Though Jamal was stronger, Trimoli was still strong. Jamal had trouble holding him down. Trimoli immediately jumped to his feet; Jamal followed him and lifted him, bringing him back to the mat. Jamal followed this with a chop and tilt, which kept him from getting to his feet momentarily. Another chop and tilt. Jamal needed back points. He couldn't get those until he got his opponent on his back. Trimoli built up and sprang to his feet again. Jamal followed Trimoli, but had trouble holding him. Trimoli worked his way forward, and Jamal followed, trying mightily to take him back down to the mat. The two reached the outer circle, and the referee blew his whistle, ending the action. They were brought back to the middle circle, and the referee set them again. Time was running out. Just :26 seconds remained.

"Far and near! Far and near!" Coach Russo yelled, shaping his hands and arms into a circle. In any other sport, an opponent could stall it out and hold onto a one-point lead. Not in wrestling. In wrestling, an opponent who is ahead by one point can't just sit there and do nothing. For ten seconds or so, a wrestler might be able to fake it, but with nearly a half of a minute left, Trimoli would have to make an effort to get away or risk giving up a point for stalling. Jamal was down by one point. A stalling point would send the match to overtime. No, Trimoli would not sit idle; he would continue to try to score.

Jamal then "got" Coach Russo's words: far and near cradle. It was a drill the team did at practice, where one wrestler was down and one was on top. On the whistle, the bottom wrestler would simulate standing with first his right foot and then his left. The top wrestler would float around the bottom wrestler applying either a far side or near side cradle, a move where the top wrestler puts one arm around the neck of his opponent and the other around his knee. He then brings the hands together, locking them, causing the other wrestler to be "cradled" up and placed on his back. Once a cradle is locked up, it is difficult to break. You may not be pinned with a cradle; you will give up back points. The move is a good counter to sit-outs and an opponent's attempts to stand. Hitting it when the other wrestler stands is sometimes tough; you have to time it perfectly.

Trimoli was set, and Jamal took his position on top. Jamal would have to be one step ahead of Trimoli to make this happen. One second off, and the match was over, as was his dream. The move would only work if Trimoli stood to his feet. If he chose to hit a move on the mat, the cradle would have to be set up with something else.

The whistle blew, and Trimoli stepped forward. Jamal was on Trimoli's right side, and when he stood with his right foot, Jamal acted, placing his right hand, the one that had been on Trimoli's elbow, on the back of Trimoli's neck. Jamal's left hand immediately went to Trimoli's right knee. Trimoli's momentum was stopped suddenly, as the cradle halted it. Trimoli found himself in awkward spot, his head and knee being forced toward each other by Jamal's grip. Trimoli was on his left side, with Jamal on his right side, trying to turn him onto his back. As he moved, Jamal pushed his head into his ribs and applied pressure. Slowly, Jamal pushed Trimoli toward his back. Twenty seconds remained. Jamal pushed, and Trimoli resisted. Jamal pressed his head harder into the ribs of Trimoli, pulling even harder on the cradle. It was too much for Trimoli. He rolled to his back, his feet in the air, and Jamal on his own hip, controlling him.

The referee signaled back points. Jamal held on until the referee blew his whistle, ending the match. Jamal was now in the finals. He won the contest 7-6. Though he didn't hold Trimoli long enough for a pin, he did hold him long enough to get a two point nearfall. Coach Russo jumped into the air, saying, "Yes!" When Jamal had his hand raised into the air, he ran to the corner, where Coach Russo gave him a big congratulatory hug. "Great job, Jamal! Now let's get that gold medal!"

Jamal felt as if he had won by one hundred points instead of just one. Victory, like Coach Russo had said, is addictive; you want it every time you go out there. Amid all the excitement of his coach and his teammates, Jamal looked into the stands. No Pop. No Mom. *They'll get here, he thought. Don't stress. Keep focused.* Hope.

— Sixteen —

Before the finals began, there was a short break. Coach Russo got the team together in a corner of the gym; he had a blue gym bag in his hand. "Look guys, take this in the locker room and change into it for the medal round. You deserve to go out in style." He began handing out the "medal round" singlets the varsity team used: solid white with a blue "K" on the chest. The varsity loved to wear the white uniforms. They were only worn for medal round matches. Jamal got his medium, and the team went to the locker room to change.

The Kennedy team had finished out the semi-final round in great shape. They had nine in the finals, with three in the consolation finals. The entire team would medal at the City Championships. It meant they had a great shot at winning the entire tournament. Kennedy sat in first place, while North High School was in second. The third and fourth place teams were close also, so getting everyone in the medal round meant little for Kennedy. Winning the city title was not a forgone conclusion.

For the consolation and championship finals, two mats had been taken up, leaving just two on the Germantown gym floor. One mat would have the third place matches, while the other would have the championship matches. Fifty-six wrestlers lined the mats, twenty-eight on one side and twenty-eight on the other side. The finals were always treated as big thing. A lot of pageantry. On each mat, fourteen wrestlers lined each side, from 103 to 285. One side had them lined up right to left, while the other side had it left to right. When the wrestler in each final's name was announced, they'd run to the center of the mat to shake each other's hand. With the way they were arranged, they didn't run straight at each other, but at an angle toward each other. When Jamal lined up up, he looked across the mat, he saw a huge 160-pound wrestler on the opposite side of the mat. He thought mistake had been made and that he would have to wrestle this guy. When his name was called, he went to the mat and saw Colin Young come towards him. They didn't make a mistake.

Oddly, Jamal didn't feel very nervous for the match. He just knew he would be nervous. Coach Russo helped. He told him the hard part was done; now was the fun part. "Just relax, and do what you do."

The 103-pound wrestlers went at it, followed by the 112-pound wrestlers. If one match ended before the other, they'd hold the next match. The organizers wanted each weight class to finish completely before the next class would get going. Made sense, Jamal thought, though it would drag things out a bit more. It was now after 7:00 PM. The tournament wouldn't be over until late. Coach Russo had told the team it might end late, and they should tell their parents it might be a late night. Parents. Where were his? It couldn't possibly take that long for a bus to travel from Chicago to downtown Memphis. *Don't stress. Keep focused.*

The finals moved at a snail's pace. With the best wrestlers in the city going at it, the matches were longer; there were no first period pins; there were a lot of coaches arguing every point. It all seemed to make the event go slower. Around 8:15 – Jamal looked at his watch in his gym bag – the 145-pound wrestlers were on the mat, and Jamal and Colin Young were warming up for their match. No Mom. *She said she'd be here. Pop said she'd be here. Don't stress. Keep focused.* Their previous two matches could not have been more different. Sure Colin Young won both of them, but he had dominated the first one. He had trouble in the second one at Christmas. Would this meeting one-month after their holiday meeting be any different? Sure Jamal was better; coach had told him so. But couldn't the same be said for Colin Young?

The 145-pound consolation match ended before the championship final did. The Kennedy wrestler at 145 had lost 6-1, but you couldn't tell by his reaction. Mark was happy that he had placed. Jamal wouldn't be happy with just placing. He wanted to win. Sure, being a first year wrestler getting to the finals was great, but winning it all was greater.

The 145 final ended. Jamal ran to the table to check in for his final. Colin Young arrived at the table just after Jamal. Neither could wait to get on the mat. "Kennedy, Hayes?" the girls keeping scored asked. When he said yes, they told him he would be wearing the green ankle band. He sprinted to the center of the mat and put on the green ankle band. He then took a knee and bowed his head. It was ritual he had picked up a few weeks earlier. Though not particularly religious when he got to Memphis, his Sundays at his grandfather's church had made an impact on him. Praying couldn't hurt. He'd seen athletes on TV do it, so he started each match with a small benediction, a little prayer that went something like, "God, help me do well, not get hurt. Don't let my opponent get hurt. Amen." He added a little to it tonight: "Help Mom get here to see me."

At the end of his "heart to heart" with "The Man," the match was ready to start. Colin Young was on his red line, and Jamal took his place on the green line. The referee looked to the head table to see if they were set. He then told Jamal and Colin to shake hands and blew his whistle. Colin moved first, a quick shot at Jamal's legs; it was more of a body fake to get Jamal leaning forward. It worked. Jamal, off balance, tied up with Young, trying to get situated and balanced. He was set up perfectly by Young.

The tie was followed by Young snapping Jamal's head down quickly, if only slightly. It was enough for Young to reach with his left hand and grab Jamal's right ankle. The head snap and the ankle pick had the still off-balance Jamal on his back, for just a second. The referee signaled the two-point takedown to the table. *Get up. Three seconds into the match, and you are already behind.* He built up to his base and stood, fighting the hands that were around his waist like a tight belt. He pushed the hands down and pushed his body forward to break free. He was soon back on the mat, belly-down with Young atop him, controlling his wrist with a two-on-one wrist ride. Jamal knew a "cheap tilt" could be done with a wrist ride, so he kept his body down and seemingly planted on the mat.

He tried to stand again, only to be taken back down to the mat. He then tried to reverse Young with a switch, but he didn't get his elbow free and was back down again. *Keep moving, Movement on the bottom. Always movement on the bottom.* Jamal sat out and reached back, hoping to find Colin's head on his right shoulder. A head roll could reverse things and even put Young on his back. The move had worked for Jamal all season. No dice. Colin Young was riding him perfectly, denying any scoring opportunity to Jamal. He couldn't turn Jamal to his back, but he as keeping Jamal on the mat and scoreless.

The first period ended with Young ahead 2-0. His North High opponent also won the choice and selected the down position. More scoring opportunities from the bottom. Colin Young was trying to increase his lead. Jamal's mind raced, the practice room suddenly reminding him of all the top wrestling he had learned: *far arm with near ankle, chop and tilt, spiral ride, follow and lift, leg rides.* The referee set Colin, and then told Jamal to take the top position. Jamal got to his position, kneeling next to Colin's left side. He placed his left knee down next to his opponent's left knee, his right hand on his opponent's belly button and his left hand on Colin's left elbow. The referee blew his whistle, starting the second period.

Young started it with a burst; he sprang to his feet. Jamal was one step ahead and took him back to the mat. Young stood again, catching Jamal off balance and scoring the one-point escape. The two wrestlers were on their feet circling each other, each looking for an opening for a takedown. Jamal was leery; he was not aggressive at all. He was playing defense. Coach Russo saw it too. “Let’s go Jamal! Turn it loose!” his coach exhorted from his chair in the corner of the mat. Jamal rushed Young, reaching for him. Bad idea. Young grabbed the arm coming at him and turned and dropped, sending Jamal sprawling. An arm drag. “Two takedown,” said the referee. Colin Young was ready for this match. More than Jamal at this point. The takedown occurred near the edge of the mat. The referee blew his whistle and brought the two back to the center circle. Jamal took his place in the down position. He was down 5-0 with just over a minute left in the second period. His head down, he looked up at the referee, whose back was to the packed bleachers behind them. The referee asked him if he was ready. Jamal said he was. Then he saw her. In the bleachers. Mom.

It was like a scene in an old movie Jamal had seen. *The Natural.* The baseball player was at the plate, bat in his hands with two strikes. He saw her. With all the people in the crowded stands that day, he somehow only saw her. The sun in the backdrop caused a bright halo, an aura, to surround her. Sun or not, he’d have seen her; he would have “sensed” her. Suddenly, she was the only person in the stands. His old flame. She was his world when they were younger; she was as vivid now as she was then. He remembered the player – Roy Hobbs, he remembered now – hit a homerun upon seeing the blonde in the hat.

The referee blew the whistle, and Jamal reacted. He was on his feet free before the last toot of the whistle had silenced. Mom. He could swear she had a halo too, even though there was no sunshine in the backdrop. She was the only person he could see, despite all the people in the stands.

The score was 5-1. Jamal circled. It was if he was a new wrestler. Whereas he was in defense mode just seconds before, he was now all aggression. He backed up Young, snapping his head down in the collar and elbow tie, pushing him around the mat. "Get out of that tie-up Jamal," ordered Coach Russo. "Get him reaching." Jamal knew exactly what coach was talking about. When your opponent reaches, then you hit the double or the single leg takedown. Jamal body-faked at Young, hoping to get him reaching. Reach he did. Double-leg takedown. "Two points takedown," said the referee. Jamal went to work. Spiral ride. Colin was flat. Jamal looked for an opening, a half nelson, anything to turn him onto his back. Nothing doing. With the score 5-3 in favor of Young, Jamal needed nearfall points to tie it or get in the lead. Young was an experienced wrestler, one who was very good at staying off his back. Jamal broke Young down when he built up to his base, but there was no opening to turn him onto his back. A bar-arm didn't work; the half didn't either. The period ended with the score at 5-3 and Jamal's choice. "Down, Jamal, down," Coach Russo said from the corner. Jamal signaled down to the referee. He took his place and looked up in the stands. He saw her again. Pop was sitting next to her. It was as if they were the only two people in the gym. He wanted to wave to let her know he saw her, but he didn't. Business at hand.

Young took his place atop Jamal. The referee blew his whistle. The final two minutes of his season had just begun. Jamal stood immediately to his feet, only to be taken back down to the mat. Young then placed all his weight on Jamal's back and grabbed his right wrist with his left hand. His right hand had slid into Jamal's elbow and was now across his back. Bar-arm tilt. Young worked to turn Jamal onto his back. Though he was unable to get him to his back, Young was able to control Jamal with the tilt. He could simply ride Jamal out and win the gold. *Get to the edge of the mat.* Jamal struggled to get to his feet, only to have his body thrown back to the mat with the tilt. It was tough to get to your feet with one arm behind your back and your opponent tripping you to the mat. He struggled and struggled from the bottom. The end line was close. Jamal could see the clock from his prone position. *One minute left.* He kept pushing his body toward the line. Each time he did, Young tightened the vise on his arm. With all his strength left, Jamal got to his feet, and Young tired to take him back down. Jamal fought the strong grip on him. He was taken back to the mat. A whistle blew. "Back to the center," the referee said. The two wrestlers went back to the center and took their spots. While Jamal was certainly tired, his opponent looked exhausted. Apparently, Young had spent all his energy keeping Jamal down. *I just need to get to my feet. Give me the energy to do it.* The whistle blew, and Jamal moved. Right to his feet he popped. He tore free. 5-4 was now the score. The clock was counting down. Forty-eight seconds left. Young would surely work the edges of the mat with a one-point lead. Jamal would have to press the action and force him to back up. Maybe the referee would hit him with a stalling point. Maybe. *Don't hope for help. Make your own way. Get that takedown!*

The two faced each other. Colin was in no hurry. He simply circled and pushed Jamal at his shoulder and head. "Dibo! Dibo! Dibo!' screamed Coach Russo. "Dibo" was not a specific move or anything, but something coach said when he wanted you to work an opponent's forehead and head, pushing at it and smacking it, setting up a double-leg takedown. Coach Russo and his words. The opponent would get so concerned with the head stuff that he'd sometimes stand tall. Young didn't bite at first. He kept a good tight stance, his butt down and his head up. "Dibo!" Jamal worked Young's head, as he backed him up. The clock was down to fifteen seconds. "Dibo!" Jamal worked Young's head, and then he hit it, his shoulder hitting Young's hips, Jamal's lead foot between Colin's squared stance. Jamal saw the clock as he lifted Colin Young in the air: :08 seconds. He barely heard the referee over the screams of the crowd, Coach Russo and his teammates. "Two takedown!" said the ref. Jamal went to the flat Young's wrist with both hands as his teammates counted down the final seconds. When the referee blew his whistle, the match was over. The score was 6-5 in favor of the Kennedy wrestler. Jamal was the 152-pound Freshman City Champion. As the referee raised his hand, he could clearly hear his mother above everyone else. Any kid might normally get a little embarrassed by such, but not Jamal and not today.

Mom can sure get loud, he thought, until he realized that she had jumped out of the bleachers and was at the mat's edge. Well, not the edge. Anna had run completely onto the mat and had her son in a huge hug. She kissed his head; she hugged him. And then repeated it. Coach Russo looked a bit confused, until he realized who this woman was who ran onto the mat.

The tournament continued on with the 160-pound wrestlers settling their issue. At the match's conclusion, it was time for the medal stand. The announcer told everyone to bring their attention to the north end of the gym for the medal presentation of the 152-pound weight class. The stand looked just like the stands Jamal had seen used at the Olympics on TV. His spot was vacant. The fourth and third place finishers took their spots on the stand. "In second place, Colin Young of North High School." Colin took his spot on the final peg before the top and bowed his head as some pretty girl from Germantown High School placed the silver medal with the red ribbon around his neck. "And now ladies and gentlemen, your Freshman City Champion at 152-pounds, Jamal Hayes!" His teammates cheered him as he ascended the medal stand. It was no more than five feet off the ground, but it might as well have been the top of Mount Everest. Jamal was on top of the world this night. Cameras flashed as he bent over to have the same pretty co-ed place the gold medal with blue ribbon around his neck. All four medalists stood for a moment for parents to get pictures. The 171-pound matches waited for the awarding ceremony to end to begin their matches. Jamal wished he could save this moment on some sort of flash-drive that he could plug into himself whenever he felt he needed a lift. *Make if last forever*, like the old song said. It was the proudest moment of his fifteen years.

Anna seemed shocked by it all. "Jamal, I can't believe what you did out there. You are really good. It's like I don't even know you. You are not my 'lil' man' anymore. You're a 'young man' now. You're so good. I can't believe it." Of course, this was said amid all the "I missed you so much-es" and the hugs. Lots of hugs.

Jamal watched the rest of the tournament with his Mom and his grandfather. Coach Russo usually wanted the team in one section together, but he understood this moment. Coach Russo could be a cool dude sometimes. As they watched the final four weight classes compete for the medals, Anna kept her arm around Jamal. If he looked in another direction, her hand would move with him. He felt a bit smothered by it, but he didn't mind at all. He was once again with the prettiest lady in the building. And she was. The stay at the "facility" had done wonders. Anna looked ten years younger. She looked more like Jamal's sister than his Mom. And he liked that.

Pop stayed silent throughout the tournament. A small smile said all that he couldn't. Contentment.

The Kennedy team won the team trophy that night, finishing just ahead of the St. Paul squad. With two weight classes missing, the Kennedy team managed to win it all: Freshmen City Champions. Coach Russo said it would take a max-effort, and he got one. Every wrestler, all twelve, placed in their weight class. Lots of hardware going back to Frayser that night.

Jamal stayed home from school the next day. Coach Russo said he would understand if he did. Pop took them out to celebrate that night. Pizza. Jamal hadn't eaten pizza since he had left Chicago. Wrestlers don't eat pizza. The three of them laughed and got themselves caught up. Anna was in great spirits, although Jamal could tell she was a bit uncertain of herself. She had told both of them that she felt like she was walking a tightrope without a net.

"Every single day will be a struggle for me. It is something I have to get used to. Once you are an addict, you're always an addict. 'One day at a time' is how I have to live. One day will turn into a week. Weeks turn into months. Before you know it, years go by, but it all starts with one day at a time." Lonny stayed quiet throughout the night, nodding his head and offering little. It was hard to tell if he was in a good mood or bad. *Poker face.*

The trio got home that night after 11 PM. Jamal was beat, as was Anna. He gladly gave up his room for his Mom; it was *her* room after all. He moved into the small room where his computer was. And was happy to do so. Mom was back.

Just before his eyes closed for the night, Pop stuck his head into Jamal's room and asked if he was awake.

"Yes sir. What is it? Anything wrong?"

"No. Just wanted to say I'm proud of what you did tonight. But not just tonight. The whole time you been here. I know I been hard on you at times. It was all worth it tonight. Seeing you out there, doing what you were doing. I ain't never been that proud of anything in my life. Maybe having my baby girl back to her old self, but you were tops. I can't tell you how proud I am of you. Good job."

He then shut the door. Jamal went to sleep the moment his head hit the pillow. He never knew contentment until that moment. It all seemed to make sense. The move, the awkward times with his grandfather, the longing for his Chicago home, the loss of his friends, the absence of his mother. It all just seemed to fit right now. Memphis was where he was supposed to be. North Memphis was home. Kennedy High School was his school, one he was proud of. Strange, feeling pride in a *school.* The last thought that entered his mind as he slipped into a deep sleep was the top of the medal stand: City Champion.

— Seventeen —

The days after the city championships were an odd mix of elation and boredom. Jamal, with no wrestling practice, found himself bored out of his mind. He asked if he could still come to practice, even though his season was over. "Sure," his coach said. "It wouldn't hurt to keep on working out. The varsity is getting ready for the region tournament and the state, but you can come out. It'll give us another body at practice. No problem. Heck, next year, you'll be on the varsity team. You'll be getting ready for the region. Might as well get a start on it now."

Jamal did practice with the team. He also continued to improve his grades. They were now back to a respectable level. In another semester or so, he might even get them back to the honor roll levels he had a long time ago.

His Mom was still doing well. She decided to stay at Pop's for a while, to figure out her next move. The doctors told her it would be better to stay there until she was ready to conquer the world alone again. *One step at a time. One day at a time.* He found himself looking forward to 6 PM each night because it meant dinnertime with his mother and Pop. Though he never said it again, Jamal could tell his grandfather enjoyed having family, *his family*, around him. It was like he got a second chance at being a young father. Though he was still demanding of Jamal and cantankerous as ever, Jamal actually felt at home in his grandfather's house. His comfort had been building since Christmas; it had only deepened since his Mom's arrival.

Anna had a job, one she took very seriously. It wasn't a great job – a clerk at a local grocery – but it was a start, a means to an end. She told Jamal that if she could prove to herself to her new boss, a new and better job could be out there. She had also gone by the University of Memphis and got an application and catalogue. She said she might start classes in the fall. She had to keep in good with her job to prove to herself that she was ready to take on more responsibilities, such as school. *One step at a time.* This was her only second chance. She was determined not to blow it.

Jamal went out for football in March. "Spring practice," said Coach Alford, "was where fall starters are made." Coach Alford was as different from Coach Russo as he could be. He was younger, probably in his early thirties. He was also black. However, the two differed little in their approach to their sports: hard work was the only way to get ahead. Jamal, it turned out, was pretty fast. He soon found his way to the second team as a safety on defense and a backup running back on offense. He liked playing defense better than offense; you got to hit people and tackle them. Playing safety was almost like wrestling in that he got to take down people. He just had to chase them and wore a lot of equipment. He struggled to get some of the language and calls of the sport – "50 Eagle," "61Strong," "Split Right 90 X Read," "I Right Over 24 Blast" – but he liked it and looked forward to the fall season. While he liked football, he viewed it as a bridge to wrestling, a way to keep busy at the start of the school year until November 1 and wrestling practice arrived.

In late April, the wrestling banquet was held. It was a swanky affair, held in the school's cafeteria. The older wrestlers told Jamal it was always a great night; Coach Russo went all out for it. There would be good food and most important, awards for the team. Coach Russo told all the wrestlers to dress nice and to bring their folks. The wrestlers would eat free, while the parents paid a nominal fee. Jamal told his mother and Pop the date and that he wanted them to be there. They said they couldn't wait.

Banquet night arrived. The school's cafeteria had been decorated like a fancy dining room. The tables had blue tablecloths on them. A head table was set up with Coach Russo at it, as well as the school's athletic director and principal. They were all in suits, including Coach Russo, who wore a blue pinstripe suit with a gold tie. He, Jamal thought, looked pretty sharp, like Mafia guys he'd seen in movies and on TV. The best of all was the table with the awards on it. It was just to side of the head table and was full of various sized plaques, trophies and medals. *Will I get anything?* Jamal thought.

The team members and their families arrived slowly but steadily for the event. When it appeared that most of the team had arrived, Coach Russo brought the dinner to order. "Wrestlers, parents, faculty and friends. It is good to have you here for the annual Kennedy Wrestling Awards Banquet. It is going to be, as usual, a great night. We got plenty of awards to give out and good food to eat. Before we get to the eats, let us give thanks for being allowed to gather on this evening. Please stand everyone." At his point, Coach Russo ceded the microphone to Reverend Alfonzo Michaels, the pastor from the Baptist church around the corner from Kennedy High School. The man was a familiar sight around the school and neighborhood. Jamal had seen him at other school events. The man dressed very sharp: black suit and red tie. He also drove a nice car; Jamal had seen it parked outside: a black Escalade. *Doing the Lord's work pays well.*

"Let us bow our heads. Dear Lord, we thank you for the opportunity to gather in fellowship tonight to celebrate with these fine young men and their coaches. By the looks of the awards, it is apparent these young men did an outstanding job during the season past. Of course, all of this glory is due to you and your word. Bless this food we are about to take in. Lord, we thank you for every single day we wake up. We thank you for the health we have. We thank you for these outstanding young men. They are our future leaders. And I have to say that I feel good about the future knowing that we are handing it off to such a fine group of young student-athletes. Amen."

Coach Russo took the microphone again. "It is time to eat. The cafeteria staff is ready to serve you. We will, just like at school, enter the lines. There are trays and silverware for you. You won't have to pay a thing for this though. I think you are going to like what we have for you. Our parents, especially our Moms, will go first, followed by the seniors and so forth. Freshmen, you'll go last." *Bottom of the food chain even at the banquet.* "Don't worry freshmen, there is plenty to eat. You'll get all you want."

All the mothers lined up and went through the buffet line that had been set up by the cafeteria staff. It didn't take long for the freshmen to get to the line. Bar-b-que. Memphis is the pork bar-b-que capital of the world. It seemed every important gathering in the city was catered by one of the area's top bar-b-que joints. There was pulled pork for sandwiches, ribs, beans, cole slaw and even bar-b-que nachos and pizza. Whatever could be made of pork bar-b-que, it was on the menu this night. Jamal got a sandwich, some beans and a few ribs. Delicious. He went back for seconds. It seemed only fitting that a wrestling banquet would be an all-you-can-eat buffet. For four months, the wresters had watched their weight. With the season done and no match or tournament on tap, eating was priority number one for the team.

While the throng dined, a huge screen was set up to the side of the tables. Videos from the past season played. There was a great mix of varsity and freshmen wrestlers on the screen, doing their thing. It turned out that Coach Russo had every event filmed and saved for this day. Many parents didn't get to see every match. This was Coach Russo's way to let them see what they missed. Each wrestler was handed an envelope when he arrived. In each was a set of 4 X 6 photos. Coach Russo took photos all year and ordered double prints so that both his scrapbook and the wrestler would each get a copy. A DVD of the season was also made available for each member of the team.

A festive atmosphere enveloped everyone in the cafeteria. The wrestlers bantered back and forth, reminiscing on the season past. Laughter followed and interrupted many conversations. Jamal sat with his other ninth grade teammates. His mother and grandfather sat near the big screen, watching the action on the screen and talking with other parents. Anna looked great in her blue dress, her hair all done. Jamal was so proud of his Mom.

Midway through the eating, the dining was interrupted by Mr. Griffith, the school's principal. "Excuse me, folks. We need to get moving with the program. From the looks of all these awards, we are going to be here awhile as it is. Don't worry, you can still eat and go back for seconds – or thirds, like I did. We will just get things started. I always enjoy these events. It is a great chance for me to boast a bit about our kids here at Kennedy. Especially our wrestlers. Without further word, parents and friends, let us give a huge round of applause for these young men. Give it up!" The entire room clapped. "Yes, do that. "We want to hear it for these outstanding young men. They deserve it." He let the applause continue. When it settled, he continued: "With so many young men, here and across the city and nation, choosing the wrong things in life, it is a pleasure to stand before you and talk about the good. And we have a lot of good in here tonight. We have a roomful of young men who choose daily to do the right thing. In the classroom and out on the mat, these young men are outstanding. They are a source of pride for me, this school and this community, something you can be proud of. We have outstanding kids on the wrestling team because we have outstanding parents who support them. Give yourselves a hand. Wrestlers, give it up for your folks!

"This team does the job. For the eighth year in a row, this team has the highest GPA of any team here at Kennedy. The team has a 95% graduation rate. Every senior on this team who will graduate this year started as a freshman four years ago. None have failed a class in that time. They are graduating on time. This is a great accomplishment. Not everyone at Kennedy does such. As the principal of Kennedy, I only wish the entire student body would wrestle; it might make them better students. Of course, it could lead to a lot of fights in the halls, fights where someone could get hurt, so maybe I don't want that." Laughter. "Seriously, this is a top-notch program, one of the best in the area, the best at this school, and we owe it to one man, Coach Russo." More applause. "Come on up, Coach Russo." More applause. "Ladies and gentleman," said Mr. Griffith, "our coach, Coach Russo!"

Coach Russo took the dais. He said thanks, and then sheepishly looked at the crowd. "I love coaching these guys. It is fun for me to see awkward and uncertain young ninth graders come into our program, only to graduate four years later confident and capable young men. It is what I do. Some people are placed on earth to build things, great things like buildings and monuments. Some are put here to write great books or paint beautiful paintings. Me, I guess I was put here to teach folks how to body-slam folks, to help shape a generation, to get young men down the road to a successful life. I've been at it a long time now, and I still get a kick out of coaching these kids in this neighborhood. Sure we have challenges that other schools don't have. Yes, we struggle to find money to keep the team. Our neighborhood is not rich, nor is our school. But since when was money the reason for any success? It isn't. Hard work is." He pointed to the awards on the table. "Take a look. Not too bad for a little school that ain't supposed to be able to compete with the larger more affluent schools. Not too bad at all." Applause.

"This year was a banner year for our team. Both the varsity and the freshman teams did an outstanding job. These two trophies show just how outstanding." He lifted up two large trophies. Coach Russo held the larger one. "This is the Region 8 Champions trophy brought home by the varsity, and this,"—he held a smaller trophy up – "is the Freshmen City Champions trophy the ninth graders won in January." More clapping. "Not too bad." He paused and let his words sink in. "At the state tournament, we did an outstanding job also. This year, our varsity squad did better than it has ever done. "We finished in the top five of the state, fourth place." Two state champions this year, with one just one match away from placing. Maybe he will win it next year." More applause. "Now, let's get to giving out these awards, the fun stuff. It'll give me another chance to brag on the boys some more."

Coach Russo started with the senior awards. Each of the seniors got a plaque, one complete with their entire high school record on it and an action photo taken at some point during the season. Next Coach Russo presented a plaque to Mr. Griffith. He also gave him two action shots of the school's two newest state champions. Jamal imagined they would go into the school's entry hallway's trophy case. He had seen other such photos in the case his first day at the school. Of course, their name would go onto the practice gym's "Wall of Fame," which was located on the wall just inside the team's practice gym. Coach Russo gave out some plaques to three parents who helped him a lot during the season. Derrick Slater's mother was one of these parents.

The next part of the program saw Coach Russo give out the team awards, the ones everyone received because the team did well. The freshman team was each called up individually to get their "City Champion" medals; the medals coach gave were much better than what the tournament gave them. Each gold medal had a blue ribbon around it with "City Champions" engraved on the back of each. Every ninth grade wrestler put it around his neck the moment he received it. The varsity team members, all twenty-two of them, each got a medal for winning a dual tournament during the regular season, a medal for a second place finish at a tournament in Chattanooga, and a gold medal for the team's first place finish in the region. Once again, each member put the medal on the moment he got it.

The "Specialty Awards" were next. Derrick Slater received a small plaque for the fastest pin that season: 11 seconds. Andre Merrick, the senior 130-pound wrestler, won the "Mr. Takedown" award, a huge trophy that had to be two feet tall; Coach Russo said that Andre had gotten 124 takedowns that season, a new school record. Derrick Slater won the "Total Team Points" award; he had scored 154 points for the varsity team that season in dual meets and tournaments. Numerous other medals and awards were given for the season. Everybody on the team had something either around their necks on in their hands; some wrestlers would need a wheelbarrow to carry out their awards. The "Most Improved Wrestler" award for the varsity and the freshman teams was given out. A few novelty-joke sort of awards were given out also. One kid on the varsity was given one boxing glove as a reward for his "knockout" during the season; he hit an ankle pick, and his opponent's head snapped back and hit the mat, causing him to black out. Another got a pair of socks, a reminder that he never had socks for the matches.

The last phase of the awards program was coming to an end. The food was running out and the awards table was getting bare. Just three awards remained on the table: two large trophies and a long box, its contents still inside. It was time to award the "Outstanding Wrestler" the "OWs" – awards to the two wrestlers selected, one from the freshmen team and one from the varsity team.

Coach Russo was back on the microphone: "Now is the big time of the night. The OW awards. These are given to the outstanding wrestler on each level. There is one for the ninth grade team and one for the varsity team. It was a hard decision to make on both counts this year. We had many outstanding competitors on each level this year, making the decision tough for the old coach. Usually it is a cut and dried process: the one who does the best gets the award. Simple. But what do you do when several do the best? You make a tough decision, but I think I got it right.

"Our freshman OW this year had an outstanding, if a somewhat surprising, season. He came out for the team a little late." Jamal started to get a knot in this stomach. *This could be me.* "He had a lot to learn and a short time to do it. But he did it. He picked up everything fast, worked hard, didn't miss a day, and rose to every challenge thrown at him." He paused. "He, in particular, met a particular challenge named Colin Young." *Colin Young? It is me.* Got beat by the kid several times, but came back and got him at the City. It was close, but he won it. Folks, our ninth grade OW, Jamal Hayes." The crowd applauded and cheered, especially Anna and even Pop. He could hear them over everyone, as he stood from his seat and walked to the front tables. He took the trophy, shook hands with Coach Russo, and then the two stood for pictures; Anna had run to the front and gotten into position to take several photos. "One more," she said, as Coach Russo and Jamal began to part. When she was finished with the photos, Anna grabbed Jamal in a big hug and smothered him again. She seemed happier than Jamal, though that was impossibility. He couldn't believe he won this award. Derrick Slater had won the same award four years earlier, and he was a two-time state champion. *Could that be me too?*

Coach Russo resumed his position at the microphone; while Jamal went to sit with his mother and Pop. "The OW for the varsity team this was a harder decision to make than the freshmen OW. I have had wrestlers win state championships before, but I have never had two in the same year. Other schools have had this happen; I've just never been fortunate enough to have that problem. I did this year." Someone had brought the long, flat box to the dais. "This year is a first. There was a tie for OW. Two state champions mean two OWs. Period." He then reached into the box and slid out two championship belts, both blue with huge gold plates on the front. "Derrick Slater and Andre Merrick. Our Outstanding Wrestlers for this year." The belts looked just like the championship belts Jamal had seen world boxing and WWE champions wear. Each belt had the recipient's name, weight class, and record on one of the side panels, and in bold letters "TSSAA State Champion" on the opposite panel. Underneath the huge, gold center plate was the writing "Kennedy OW." Coach Russo had the belts special made each year. You could tell he enjoyed giving out the awards as much or more than those who received them. He took pictures with both of the senior wrestlers. They each held their belts up for the photos. Andre said, in jest, "Maybe we should push all the tables aside and wrestle to see who should really get the OW belt." It was a happy night, something Jamal had never come to expect from anything school-related. He had never received an award of any type; he couldn't describe how he felt. His mother was overjoyed. Pop was proud, holding and examining Jamal's trophy. A good night, for sure.

"Just one more award, our 'Top Student/Wrestler Award,' probably the most important award we give out. After all, school is why we are all here." Let the thought sink in. "Our top student/wrestler this year is a top notch student, top wrestler and, more importantly, a grade-A person. He also won this award last year. And to think that I remember when he was a scrawny ninth-grader in the office for fighting. Now, look at him—a 3.8 student, two-time state champion and a potential college wrestler. Two schools, one from the Ivy League and the other – Northwestern – from the Big Ten, have shown an interest in signing one of our very own. An outstanding young man, one I am so proud to have coached – Derrick Slater!" Applause. Standing ovation. Derrick's mother grabbed Coach Russo by the neck, as she hugged her son Derrick. Derrick, with all his medals, belt and other trophies, was decorated like a war veteran. He was taking a lot of "hardware" home with him tonight.

All Jamal could think was, *that's gonna' be me next year.*

After handing out the OW belts and the Top Student/Wrestler award, Mr. Griffith took the microphone: "We are about done folks, but before we go, let's have another round of applause for these outstanding young men and for Coach Russo. I never get tired of these sorts of events, and the wrestling team gives Kennedy more than its share of such. Coach, you and the team get up here in the front, come on." The team got out of their seats and walked to the front table, where Coach Russo stood. "Let's hear it for them folks. An outstanding job." Parents and friends got up and took pictures of the team and its coach.

Coach Russo was speaking with parents as they gathered their belongings to leave. Every parent, it seemed, shook his hand and wished him well. Some parents took pictures with coach. Every returning wrestler told coach to go ahead and put his name on the belt for next year. Anna waited her turn. She shook Coach Russo's hand, and then grabbed his neck with a huge hug. Jamal could hear what she was saying: "I thank you so much for all the help you gave Jamal. So much. He has come to respect you so much, and I don't know what would have happened with him had he not gotten involved with wrestling. I can't tell you how much I appreciate all you did for Jamal. And you can bet he will be there next year –"

Coach Russo interrupted her: "I thought the two of you might be heading back to Chicago."

"No sir. Not any time soon. We will be here for the foreseeable future."

Jamal liked hearing that. His days of missing Chicago were done. He had business to take care of at Kennedy High School. He had a new life now, one that he enjoyed; he had friends, his teammates, and he had some goals for himself. New territory.

Pop had been standing quietly behind his daughter. He stood forward and grabbed Coach Russo's hand. "Good job, coach. I think you got the boy's mind right, thinking the right stuff. I'm glad I let him do this stuff. I still don't get all of it, but it looks like it works. You do some good stuff for the kids in this neighborhood. Next year, I want to help however I can. I don't know nothing about coaching or anything, but I can do a bunch of stuff. Might be able to help out."

"Mr. Hayes, I am sure there is plenty you can do. We are thinking of starting a booster club. We'll need some leadership on that. I bet you could do a great job. I'll be in touch."

"You do that, coach. You do that."

The three of them, "Jamal's family," headed out to the parking lot, Anna holding Jamal's trophy in one hand and her "trophy" – Jamal – with the other.

As they drove home, Jamal looked over to his grandfather and asked, "Pop, do you still know how to box?"

"Of course not. I done that years ago. Why?"

"I'm gonna' have to stay busy until wrestling starts. Thought I might give boxing a go."

I don't know, boy. We'll see."

— Eighteen —

As part of an end of year writing assignment, Jamal's English class had to write an essay entitled "What I Learned This School Year." Jamal's would not be easy to write; he had learned so much. Where would he start?

He stared at his keyboard and computer screen, pondering how to start his essay. Then he began:

"I learned so much this school year. It is difficult to say which was the most important. I guess I learned a lot from wrestling. I had never done a sport in my life until I walked into the Kennedy wrestling gym. I learned so much in there. Sure, I learned a bunch of wrestling moves, but I also learned so much more. I discovered that you got to keep on going and that you can't ever quit. Sometimes life doesn't go like you want it to go, but you can't quit. I learned that when you get knocked down, it is so important to get right up and go right back at it. If something is difficult, I learned that you have to keep on working at figuring it all out. I learned that defeat doesn't last forever; it is only temporary. There is always a brand new day. I learned that you have to show up every day. Life doesn't allow you take a day off. I learned that if you show up every day and work, then good things will happen. They might not happen right away, but they will never happen if you don't work. I learned that being tough is much more than beating someone up. There is something called being mentally tough. This is being able to handle disappointment and not falling apart the first time things go bad. I guess what I am trying to say is that you have to keep going and never ever quit. It doesn't matter if it is a sport like wrestling or if it is in a certain class like math: you have to keep trying. There's an old saying – 'When the going gets tough, the tough get going.' This is so true. As Coach Russo told us, 'Tough times don't last; tough people do.' I think I have gotten tougher as a person and not just as a wrestler or athlete. I hope I can remember to keep on going when things don't go so well or like I want. I hope when I am my grandfather's age, I am as tough-minded as he is. Though he never wrestled, he learned that lesson somewhere. 'Perseverance' is a word I learned this year in English. I hope this is what I have learned this school year. I want to be like the quote my history teacher has on his wall; it is from Winston Churchill, who was a leader in England a long time ago. The quote goes: 'When you're going through hell, keep going.' It's been a tough year for me in a lot of ways. I have been through 'hell' in a way, but I kept on going. I kept on working. That is what I have learned."

-- Jamal Hayes, English 9